Isobel

James Oliver Curwood

Contents

ISOBEL

BY

James Oliver Curwood

TO
CARLOTTA
WHO IS WITH ME AND TO
VIOLA
WHO FILLS FOR ME A DREAM OF THE FUTURE
I AFFECTIONATELY DEDICATE THIS BOOK

I
THE MOST TERRIBLE THING IN THE WORLD

At Point Fullerton, one thousand miles straight north of civilization, Sergeant William MacVeigh wrote with the stub end of a pencil between his fingers the last words of his semi-annual report to the Commissioner of the Royal Northwest Mounted Police at Regina. He concluded:

"I beg to say that I have made every effort to run down Scottie Deane, the murderer. I have not given up hope of finding him, but I believe that he has gone from my territory and is probably now somewhere within the limits of the Fort Churchill patrol. We have hunted the country for three hundred miles south along the shore of Hudson's Bay to Eskimo Point, and as far north as Wagner Inlet. Within three months we have made three patrols west of the Bay, unraveling sixteen hundred miles without finding our man or word of him. I respectfully advise a close watch of the patrols south of the Barren Lands."

"There!" said MacVeigh aloud, straightening his rounded shoulders with a groan of relief. "It's done."

From his bunk in a corner of the little wind and storm beaten cabin which represented Law at the top end of the earth Private Pelliter lifted a head wearily from his sick bed and said: "I'm bloomin' glad of it, Mac. Now mebbe you'll give me a drink of water and shoot that devilish huskie that keeps howling every now and then out there as though death was after me."

"Nervous?" said MacVeigh, stretching his strong young frame with another sigh of satisfaction. "What if you had to write this twice a year?" And he pointed at the report.

"It isn't any longer than the letters you wrote to that girl of yours--"

Pelliter stopped short. There was a moment of embarrassing silence. Then he added, bluntly, and with a hand reaching out: "I beg your pardon, Mac. It's this fever. I forgot for a moment that-- that you two-- had broken."

"That's all right," said MacVeigh, with a quiver in his voice, as he turned for the water.

"You see," he added, returning with a tin cup, "this report is different. When you're writing to the Big Mogul himself something gets on your nerves. And it has been a bad year with us, Pelly. We fell down on Scottie, and let the raiders from that whaler get away from us. And-- By Jo, I forgot to mention the wolves!"

"Put in a P. S.," suggested Pelliter.

"A P. S. to his Royal Nibs!" cried MacVeigh, staring incredulously at his mate. "There's no use of feeling your pulse any more, Pelly. The fever's got you. You're sure out of your head."

He spoke cheerfully, trying to bring a smile to the other's pale face. Pelliter dropped back with a sigh.

"No-- there isn't any use feeling my pulse," he repeated. "It isn't sickness, Bill-- not sickness of the ordinary sort. It's in my brain-- that's where it is. Think of it-- nine months up here, and never a glimpse of a white man's face except yours. Nine months without the sound of a woman's voice. Nine months of just that dead, gray world out there, with the northern lights hissing at us every night like snakes and the black rocks staring at us as they've stared for a million centuries. There may be glory in it, but that's all. We're 'eroes all right, but there's no one knows it but ourselves and the six hundred and forty-nine other men of the Royal Mounted. My God, what I'd give for the sight of a girl's face, for just a moment's touch of her hand! It would drive out this fever, for it's the fever of loneliness, Mac-- a sort of madness, and it's splitting my 'ead."

"Tush, tush!" said MacVeigh, taking his mate's hand. "Wake up, Pelly! Think of what's coming. Only a few months more of it, and we'll be changed. And then-- think of what a heaven you'll be entering. You'll be able to enjoy it more than the other fellows, for they've never had this. And I'm going to bring you back a letter-- from the little girl--"

Pelliter's face brightened.

"God bless her!" he exclaimed. "There'll be letters from her-- a dozen of them. She's waited a long time for me, and she's true to the bottom of her dear heart. You've got my letter safe?"

"Yes."

MacVeigh went back to the rough little table and added still further to his re-por

"Pelliter is sick with a strange trouble in his head. At times I
have been afraid he was going mad, and if he lives I advise his
transfer south at an early date. I am leaving for Churchill two
weeks ahead of the usual time in order to get medicines. I also
wish to add a word to what I said about wolves in my last report.
We have seem them repeatedly in packs of from fifty to one
thousand. Late this autumn a pack attacked a large herd of
traveling caribou fifteen miles in from the Bay, and we counted the
remands of one hundred and sixty animals killed over a distance of
less than three miles. It is my opinion that the wolves kill at
least five thousand caribou in this patrol each year.

"I have the honor to be, sir,

"Your obedient servant,
" WILLIAM MACVEIGH, Sergeant,
"In charge of detachment."

He folded the report, placed it with other treasures in the waterproof rubber bag which always went into his pack, and returned to Pelliter's side.

"I hate to leave you alone, Pelly," he said. "But I'll make a fast trip of it-- four hundred and fifty miles over the ice, and I'll do it in ten days or bust. Then ten days back, mebbe two weeks, and you'll have the medicines and the letters. Hurrah!"

"Hurrah!" cried Pelliter.

He turned his face a little to the wall. Something rose up in MacVeigh's throat and choked him as he gripped Pelliter's hand.

"My God, Bill, is that the sun ?" suddenly cried Pelliter.

MacVeigh wheeled toward the one window of the cabin. The sick man tumbled from his bunk. Together they stood for a moment at the window, staring far to the south and east, where a faint red rim of gold shot up through the leaden sky.

"It's the sun," said MacVeigh, like one speaking a prayer.

"The first in four months," breathed Pelliter.

Like starving men the two gazed through the window. The golden light lingered for a few moments, then died away. Pelliter went back to his bunk.

Half an hour later four dogs, a sledge, and a man were moving swiftly through the dead and silent gloom of Arctic day. Sergeant MacVeigh was on his way to Fort Churchill, more than four hundred miles away.

This is the loneliest journey in the world, the trip down from the solitary little wind-beaten cabin at Point Fullerton to Fort Churchill. That cabin has but one rival in the whole of the Northland-- the other cabin at Herschel Island, at the mouth of the Firth, where twenty-one wooden crosses mark twenty-one white men's graves. But whalers come to Herschel. Unless by accident, or to break the laws, they never come in the neighborhood of Fullerton. It is at Fullerton that men die of the most terrible thing in the world-- loneliness. In the little cabin men have gone mad.

The gloomy truth oppressed MacVeigh as he guided his dog team over the ice into the south. He was afraid for Pelliter. He prayed that Pelliter might see the sun now and then. On the second day he stopped at a cache of fish which they had put up in the early autumn for dog feed. He stopped at a second cache on the fifth day, and spent the sixth night at an Eskimo igloo at Blind Eskimo Point. Late en the ninth day he came into Fort Churchill, with an average of fifty miles a day to his credit.

From Fullerton men came in nearer dead than alive when they made the hazard in winter. MacVeigh's face was raw from the beat of the wind. His eyes were red. He had a touch of runner's cramp. He slept for twenty-four hours in a warm bed without stirring. When he awoke he raged at the commanding officer of the barrack for letting him sleep so long, ate three meals in one, and did up his business in a hurry.

His heart warmed with pleasure when he sorted out of his mail nine letters for Pelliter, all addressed in the same small, girlish hand. There was none for himself-- none of the sort which Pelliter was receiving, and the sickening loneliness within him grew almost suffocating.

He laughed softly as he broke a law. He opened one of Pelliter's letters-- the last one written-- and calmly read it. It was filled with the sweet tenderness of a girl's love, and tears came into his red eyes. Then he sat down and answered it. He told the girl about Pelliter, and confessed to her that he had opened her last letter. And the chief of what he said was that it would be a glorious surprise to a man who was going mad (only he used loneliness in place of madness) if she would come up to Churchill the following spring and marry him there. He told her that he had opened her letter because he loved Pelliter more than most men loved their brothers. Then he resealed the letter, gave his mail to the superintendent, packed his medicines and supplies, and made ready to return.

On this same day there came into Churchill a halfbreed who had been hunting white foxes near Blind Eskimo, and who now and then did scout work for the department. He brought the information that he had seen a white man and a white woman ten miles south of the Maguse River. The news thrilled MacVeigh.

"I'll stop at the Eskimo camp," he said to the superintendent. "It's worth investigating, for I never knew of a white woman north of sixty in this country. It might be Scottie Deane."

"Not very likely," replied the superintendent. "Scottie is a tall man, straight and powerful. Coujag says this man was no taller than himself, and walked like a hunchback. But if there are white people out there their history is worth knowing."

The following morning MacVeigh started north. He reached the half-dozen igloos which made up the Eskimo village late the third day. Bye-Bye, the chief man, offered him no encouragement, MacVeigh gave him a pound of bacon, and in return for the magnificent present Bye-Bye told him that he had seen no white people. MacVeigh gave him another pound, and Bye-Bye added that he had not heard of any white people. He listened with the lifeless stare of a walrus while MacVeigh impressed upon him that he was going inland the next morning to search for white people whom he had heard were there. That night, in a blinding snow-storm, Bye-Bye disappeared from camp.

MacVeigh left his dogs to rest up at the igloo village and swung northwest on snow-shoes with the break of arctic dawn, which was but little better than the night itself. He planned to continue in this direction until he struck the Barren, then patrol in a wide circle that would bring him back to the Eskimo camp the next night. From the first he was handicapped by the storm. He lost Bye-Bye's snow-shoe tracks a hundred yards from the igloos. All that day he searched in sheltered places for signs of a camp or trail. In the afternoon the wind died away, the sky cleared, and in the wake of the calm the cold became so intense that trees cracked with reports like pistol shots.

He stopped to build a fire of scrub bush and eat his supper on the edge of the Barren just as the cold stars began blazing over his head. It was a white, still night. The southern timberline lay far behind him, and to the north there was no timber for three hundred miles. Between those lines there was no life, and so there was no sound. On the west the Barren thrust itself down in a long finger ten miles in width, and across that MacVeigh would have to strike to reach the wooded country beyond. It was over there that he had the greatest hope of discovering a trail. After he had finished his supper he loaded his pipe, and sat hunched close up to his fire, staring out over the Barren. For some reason he was filled with a strange and uncomfortable emotion, and he wished that he had brought along one of his tired dogs to keep him company.

He was accustomed to loneliness; he had laughed in the face of things that had driven other men mad. But to-night there seemed to be something about him that he had never known before, something that wormed its way deep down into his soul and made his pulse beat faster. He thought of Pelliter on his fever bed, of Scottie Deane, and then of himself. After all, was there much to choose between the three of them?

A picture rose slowly before him in the bush-fire, and in that picture he saw Scottie, the man-hunted man, fighting a great fight to keep himself from being hung by the neck until he was dead; and then he saw Pelliter, dying of the sickness which comes of loneliness, and beyond those two, like a pale cameo appearing for a moment out of gloom, he saw the picture of a face. It was a girl's face, and it was gone in an instant. He had hoped against hope that she would write to him again. But she had failed him.

He rose to his feet with a little laugh, partly of joy and partly of pain, as he thought of the true heart that was waiting for Pelliter. He tied on his snow-shoes and struck out over the Barren. He moved swiftly, looking sharply ahead of him. The night grew brighter, the stars more brilliant. The zipp, zipp, zipp of the tails of his snow-shoes was the only sound he heard except the first faint, hissing monotone of the aurora in the northern skies, which came to him like the shivering run of steel sledge runners on hard snow.

In place of sound the night about him began to fill with ghostly life. His shadow beckoned and grimaced ahead of him, and the stunted bush seemed to move. His eyes were alert and questing. Within himself he reasoned that he would see nothing, and yet some unusual instinct moved him to caution. At regular intervals he stopped to listen and to sniff the air for an odor of smoke. More and more he became like a beast of prey. He left the last bush behind him. Ahead of him the starlit space was now unbroken by a single shadow. Weird whispers came with a low wind that was gathering in the north.

Suddenly MacVeigh stopped and swung his rifle into the crook of his arm. Something that was not the wind had come up out of the night. He lifted his fur cap from his ears and listened. He heard it again, faintly, the frosty singing of sledge runners. The sledge was approaching from the open Barren, and he cleared for action. He took off his heavy fur mittens and snapped them to his belt, replaced them with his light service gloves, and examined his revolver to see that the cylinder was not frozen. Then he stood silent and waited.

II
BILLY MEETS THE WOMAN

Out of the gloom a sledge approached slowly. It took form at last in a dim shadow, and MacVeigh saw that it would pass very near to him. He made out, one after another, a human figure, three dogs, and the toboggan. There was something appalling in the quiet of this specter of life looming up out of the night. He could no longer hear the sledge, though it was within fifty paces of him. The figure in advance walked slowly and with bowed head, and the dogs and the sledge followed in a ghostly line. Human leader and animals were oblivious to MacVeigh, silent and staring in the white night. They were opposite him before he moved.

Then he strode out quickly, with a loud holloa. At the sound of his voice there followed a low cry, the dogs stopped in their traces, and the figure ran back to the sledge. MacVeigh drew his revolver. Half a dozen long strides and he had reached the sledge. From the opposite side a white face stared at him, and with one hand resting on the heavily laden sledge, and his revolver at level with his waist, MacVeigh stared back in speechless astonishment.

For the great, dark, frightened eyes that looked across at him, and the white, staring face he recognized as the eyes and the face of a woman. For a moment he was unable to move or speak, and the woman raised her hands and pushed back her fur hood so that he saw her hair shimmering in the starlight. She was a white woman. Suddenly he saw something in her face that struck him with a chill, and he looked down at the thing under his hand. It was a long, rough box. He drew back a step.

"Good God!" he said. "Are you alone?"

She bowed her head, and he heard her voice in a half sob.

"Yes-- alone."

He passed quickly around to her side. "I am Sergeant MacVeigh, of the Royal Mounted," he said, gently. "Tell me, where are you going, and how does it happen that you are out here in the Barren-- alone."

Her hood had fallen upon her shoulder, and she lifted her face full to MacVeigh. The stars shone in her eyes. They were wonderful eyes, and now they were filled with pain. And it was a wonderful face to MacVeigh, who had not seen a white woman's face for nearly a year. She was young, so young that in the pale glow of the night she looked almost like a girl, and in her eyes and mouth and the upturn of her chin there was something so like that other face of which he had dreamed that he reached out and took her two hesitating hands in his own, and asked again:

"Where are you going, and why are you out here-- alone?"

"I am going-- down there," she said, turning her head toward the timber-line. "I am going with him-- my husband--"

Her voice choked her, and, drawing her hands suddenly from him, she went to the sledge and stood facing him. For a moment there was a glow of defiance in her eyes, as though she feared him and was ready to fight for herself and her dead. The dogs slunk in at her feet, and MacVeigh saw the gleam of their naked fangs in the starlight.

"He died three days ago," she finished, quietly, "and I am taking him back to my people, down on the Little Seul."

"It is two hundred miles," said MacVeigh, looking at her as if she were mad. "You will die."

"I have traveled two days," replied the woman. "I am going on."

"Two days-- across the Barren!"

MacVeigh looked at the box, grim and terrible in the ghostly radiance that fell upon it. Then he looked at the woman. She had bowed her head upon her breast, and her shining hair fell loose and disheveled. He saw the pathetic droop of her tired shoulders, and knew that she was crying. In that moment a thrilling warmth flooded every fiber of his body, and the glory of this that had come to him from out of the Barren held him mute. To him woman was all that was glorious and good. The pitiless loneliness of his life had placed them next to angels in his code of things, and before him now he saw all that he had ever dreamed of in the love and loyalty of womanhood and of wifehood.

The bowed little figure before him was facing death for the man she had loved, and who was dead. In a way he knew that she was mad. And yet her madness was the madness of a devotion that was beyond fear, of a faithfulness that made no measure of storm and cold and starvation; and he was filled with a desire to go up to her as she stood crumpled and exhausted against the box, to take her close in his arms and tell her that of such a love he had built for himself the visions which had kept him alive in his loneliness. She looked pathetically like a child.

"Come, little girl," he said. "We'll go on. I'll see you safely on your way to the Little Seul. You mustn't go alone. You'd never reach your people alive. My God, if I were he--"

He stopped at the frightened look in the white face she lifted to him.

"What?" she asked.

"Nothing-- only it's hard for a man to die and lose a woman like you," said MacVeigh. "There-- let me lift you up on the box."

"The dogs cannot pull the load," she objected. "I have helped them--"

"If they can't, I can," he laughed, softly; and with a quick movement he picked her up and seated her on the sledge. He stripped off his pack and placed it behind her, and then he gave her his rifle. The woman looked straight at him with a tense, white face as she placed the weapon across her lap.

"You can shoot me if I don't do my duty," said MacVeigh. He tried to hide the happiness that came to him in this companionship of woman, but it trembled in his voice. He stopped suddenly, listening.

"What was that?"

"I heard nothing," said the woman. Her face was deadly white. Her eyes had grown black.

MacVeigh turned, with a word to the dogs. He picked up the end of the babiche rope with which the woman had assisted them to drag their load, and set off across the Barren. The presence of the dead had always been oppressive to him, but to-night it was otherwise. His fatigue of the day was gone, and in spite of the thing he was helping to drag behind him he was filled with a strange elation. He was in the presence of a woman. Now and then he turned his head to look at her. He could feel her behind him, and the sound of her low voice when she spoke to the dogs was like music to him. He wanted to burst forth in the wild song with which he and Pelliter had kept up their courage in the little cabin, but he throttled his desire and whistled instead. He wondered how the woman and the dogs had dragged the sledge. It sank deep in the soft drift-snow, and taxed his strength. Now and then he paused to rest, and at last the woman jumped from the sledge and came to his side.

"I am going to walk," she said. "The load is too heavy."

"The snow is soft," replied MacVeigh. "Come."

He held out his hand to her; and, with the same strange, white look in her face, the woman gave him her own. She glanced back uneasily toward the box, and MacVeigh understood. He pressed her fingers a little tighter and drew her nearer to him. Hand in hand, they resumed their way across the Barren. MacVeigh said nothing, but his blood was running like fire through his body. The little hand he held trembled and started uneasily. Once or twice it tried to draw itself away, and he held it closer. After that it remained submissively in his own, warm and thrilling. Looking down, he could see the profile of the woman's face.

A long, shining tress of her hair had freed itself from under her hood, and the light wind lifted it so that it fell across his arm. Like a thief he raised it to his lips, while the woman looked straight ahead to where the timber-line began to show in a thin, black streak. His cheeks burned, half with shame, half with tumultuous joy. Then he straightened his shoulders and shook the floating tress from his arm.

Three-quarters of an hour later they came to the first of the timber. He still held her hand. He was still holding it, with the brilliant starlight falling upon them, when his chin shot suddenly into the air again, alert and fighting, and he cried, softly:

"What was that?"

"Nothing," said the woman. "I heard nothing-- unless it was the wind in the trees."

She drew away from him. The dogs whined and slunk close to the box. Across the Barren came a low, wailing wind.

"The storm is coming back," said MacVeigh. "It must have been the wind that I heard."

III
IN HONOR OF THE LIVING

For a few moments after uttering those words Billy stood silent listening for a sound that was not the low moaning of the wind far out on the Barren. He was sure that he had heard it-- something very near, almost at his feet, and yet it was a sound which he could not place or understand. He looked at the woman. She was gazing steadily at him.

"I hear it now," she said. "It is the wind. It has frightened me. It makes such terrible sounds at times-- out on the Barren. A little while ago-- I thought-- I heard-- a child crying--"

Billy saw her clutch a hand at her throat, and there were both terror and grief in the eyes that never for an instant left his face. He understood. She was almost ready to give way under the terrible strain of the Barren. He smiled at her, and spoke in a voice that he might have used to a little child.

"You are tired, little girl?"

"Yes-- yes-- I am tired--"

"And hungry and cold?"

"Yes."

"Then we will camp in the timber."

They went on until they came to a growth of spruce so dense that it formed a shelter from both snow and wind, with a thick carpet of brown needles under foot. They were shut out from the stars, and in the darkness MacVeigh began to whistle cheerfully. He unstrapped his pack and spread out one of his blankets close to the box and wrapped the other about the woman's shoulders.

"You sit here while I make a fire," he said.

He piled up dry needles over a precious bit of his birchbark and struck a flame.

In the glowing light he found other fuel, and added to the fire until the crackling blaze leaped as high as his head. The woman's face was hidden, and she looked as though she had fallen asleep in the warmth of the fire. For half an hour Mac-Veigh dragged in fuel until he had a great pile of it in readiness.

Then he forked out a deep bed of burning coals and soon the odor of coffee and frying bacon aroused his companion. She raised her head and threw back the blanket with which he had covered her shoulders. It was warm where she sat, and she took off her hood while he smiled at her companionably from over the fire. Her reddish-brown hair tumbled about her shoulders, rippling and glistening in the fire glow, and for a few moments she sat with it falling loosely about her, with her eyes upon MacVeigh. Then she gathered it between her fingers, and MacVeigh watched her while she divided it into shining strands and pleated it into a big braid.

"Supper is ready," he said. "Will you eat it there?"

She nodded, and for the first time she smiled at him. He brought bacon and bread and coffee and other things from his pack and placed them on a folded blanket between them. He sat opposite her, cross-legged. For the first time he noticed that her eyes were blue and that there was a flush in her cheeks. The flush deepened as he looked at her, and she smiled at him again.

The smile, the momentary drooping of her eyes, set his heart leaping, and for a little while he was unconscious of taste in the food he swallowed. He told her of his post away up at Point Fullerton, and of Pelliter, who was dying of loneliness.

"It's been a long time since I've seen a woman like you," he confided. "And it seems like heaven. You don't know how lonely I am!" His voice trembled. "I wish that Pelliter could see you-- just for a moment," he added. "It would make him live again."

Something in the soft glow of her eyes urged other words to his lips.

"Mebbe you don't know what it means not to see a white woman in-- in-- all this time," he went on. "You won't think that I've gone mad, will you, or that I'm saying or doing anything that's wrong? I'm trying to hold myself back, but I feel like shouting, I'm that glad. If Pelliter could see you--" He reached suddenly in his pocket and drew out the precious packet of letters. "He's got a girl down south-- just like you," he said. "These are from her. If I get 'em up in time they'll bring him round. It's not medicine he wants. It's woman-- just a sight of her, and sound of her, and a touch of her hand."

She reached across and took the letters. In the firelight he saw that her hand was trembling.

"Are they-- married?" she asked, softly.

"No, but they're going to be," he cried, triumphantly. "She's the most beautiful thing in the world, next to--"

He paused, and she finished for him.

"Next to one other girl-- who is yours."

"No, I wasn't going to say that. You won't think I mean wrong, will you, if I tell you? I was going to say next to-- you. For you've come out of the blizzard-- like an angel to give me new hope. I was sort of broke when you came. If you disappeared now and I never saw you again I'd go back and fight the rest of my time out, an' dream of pleasant things. Gawd! Do you know a man has to be put up here before he knows that life isn't the sun an' the moon an' the stars an' the air we breathe. It's woman-- just woman."

He was returning the letters to his pocket. The woman's voice was clear and gentle. To Billy it rose like sweetest music above the crackling of the fire and the murmuring of the wind in the spruce tops.

"Men like you-- ought to have a woman to care for," she said. "He was like that."

"You mean--" His eyes sought the long, dark box.

"Yes-- he was like that."

"I know how you feel," he said; and for a moment he did not look at her. "I've gone through-- a lot of it. Father an' mother and a sister. Mother was the last, and I wasn't much more than a kid-- eighteen, I guess-- but it don't seem much more than yesterday. When you come up here and you don't see the sun for months nor a white face for a year or more it brings up all those things pretty much as though they happened only a little while ago.'"

"All of them are-- dead?" she asked.

"All but one. She wrote to me for a long time, and I thought she'd keep her word. Pelly-- that's Pelliter-- thinks we've just had a misunderstanding, and that she'll write again. I haven't told him that she turned me down to marry another fellow. I didn't want to make him think any unpleasant things about his own girl.

You're apt to do that when you're almost dying of loneliness."

The woman's eyes were shining. She leaned a little toward him.

"You should be glad," she said. "If she turned you down she wouldn't have been worthy of you-- afterward. She wasn't a true woman. If she had been, her love wouldn't have grown cold because you were away. It mustn't spoil your faith-- because that is-- beautiful."

He had put a hand into his pocket again, and drew out now a thin package wrapped in buckskin. His face was like a boy's.

"I might have-- if I hadn't met you," he said. "I'd like to let you know-- some way-- what you've done for me. You and this."

He had unfolded the buckskin, and gave it to her. In it were the big blue petals and dried, stem of a blue flower.

"A blue flower!" she said.

"Yes. You know what it means. The Indians call it i-o-waka, or something like that, because they believe that it is the flower spirit of the purest and most beautiful thing in the world. I have called it woman."

He laughed, and there was a joyous sort of note in the laugh.

"You may think me a little mad," he said, "but do you care if I tell you about that blue flower?"

The woman nodded. There was a little quiver at her throat which Billy did not see.

"I was away up on the Great Bear," he said, "and for ten days and ten nights I was in camp-- alone-- laid up with a sprained ankle. It was a wild and gloomy place, shut in by barren ridge mountains, with stunted black spruce all about, and those spruce were haunted by owls that made my blood run cold nights. The second day I found company. It was a blue flower. It grew close to my tent, as high as my knee, and during the day I used to spread out my blanket close to it and lie there and smoke. And the blue flower would wave on its slender stem, an' bob at me, an' talk in sign language that I imagined I understood. Sometimes it was so funny and vivacious that I laughed, and then it seemed to be inviting me to a dance. And at other times it was just beautiful and still, and seemed listening to what the forest was saying-- and once or twice, I thought, it might be praying. Loneliness makes a fellow foolish, you know. With the going of the sun my blue flower would always fold its petals and go to sleep, like a little child tired out by the day's play, and after that I would feel terribly lonely. But it was always awake again when I rolled out in the morning. At last the time came when I was well enough to leave. On the ninth night I watched my blue flower go to sleep for the last time. Then I packed. The sun was up when I went away the next morning, and from a little distance I turned and looked back. I suppose I was foolish, and weak for a man, but I felt like crying. Blue flower had taught me many things I had not known before. It had made me think. And when I looked back it was in a pool of sunlight, and it was waving at me! It seemed to me that it was calling-- calling me back-- and I ran to it and picked it from the stem, and it has been with me ever since that hour. It has been my Bible an' my comrade, an' I've known it was the spirit of the purest and the most beautiful thing in the world-- woman. I--" His voice broke a little. "I-- I may be foolish, but I'd like to have you take it, an' keep it-- always-- for me."

He could see now the quiver of her lips as she looked across at him.

"Yes, I will take it," she said. "I will take it and keep it-- always."

"I've been keeping it for a woman-- somewhere," he said. "Foolish idea, wasn't it? And I've been telling you all this, when I want to hear what happened back there, and what you are going to do when you reach your people. Do you mind-- telling me?"

"He died-- that's all," she replied, fighting to speak calmly. "I promised to take him back-- to my people, And when I get there-- I don't know-- what I shall-- do--"

She caught her breath. A low sob broke from her lips.

"You don't know-- what you will do--"

Billy's voice sounded strange even to himself. He rose to his feet and looked down into her upturned face, his hands clenched, his body trembling with the fight he was making. Words came to his lips and were forced back again-- words which almost won in their struggle to tell her again that she had come to him from out of the Barren like an angel, that within the short space since their meeting he had lived a lifetime, and that he loved her as no man had ever loved a woman before. Her blue eyes looked at him questioningly as he stood above her.

And then he saw the thing which for a moment he had forgotten-- the long, rough box at the woman's back. His fingers dug deeper into his palms, and with a gasping breath he turned away. A hundred paces back in the spruce he had found a bare rock with a red bakneesh vine growing over it. With his knife he cut off an armful, and when he returned with it into the light of the fire the bakneesh glowed like a mass of crimson flowers. The woman had risen to her feet, and looked at him speechlessly as he scattered the vine over the box. He turned to her and said, softly:

"In honor of the dead!"

The color had faded from her face, but her eyes shone like stars. Billy advanced toward her with his hands reaching out. But suddenly he stopped and stood listening. After a moment he turned and asked again:

"What was that?"

"I heard the dogs-- and the wind," she replied.

"It's something cracking in my head, I guess," said MacVeigh. "It sounded like--" He passed a hand over his forehead and looked at the dogs huddled in deep sleep beside the sledge. The woman did not see the shiver that passed through him. He laughed cheerfully, and seized his ax.

"Now for the camp," he announced. "We're going to get the storm within an hour."

On the box the woman carried a small tent, and he pitched it close to the fire, filling the interior two feet deep with cedar and balsam boughs. His own silk service tent he put back in the deeper shadows of the spruce. When he had finished he looked questioningly at the woman and then at the box.

"If there is room-- I would like it in there-- with me," she said, and while she stood with her face to the fire he dragged the box into the tent. Then he piled fresh fuel upon the fire and came to bid her good night. Her face was pale and haggard now, but she smiled at him, and to MacVeigh she was the most beautiful thing in the world. Within himself he felt that he had known her for years and years, and he took her hands and looked down into her blue eyes and said, almost in a whisper:

"Will you forgive me if I'm doing wrong? You don't know how lonesome I've been, and how lonesome I am, and what it means to me to look once more into a woman's face. I don't want to hurt you, and I'd-- I'd"-- his voice broke a little--"I'd give him back life if I could, just because I've seen you and know you and-- and love you."

She started and drew a quick, sharp breath that came almost in a low cry.

"Forgive me, little girl," he went on. "I may be a little mad. I guess I am. But I'd die for you, and I'm going to see you safely down to your people-- and-- and-- I wonder-- I wonder-- if you'd kiss me good night--"

Her eyes never left his face. They were dazzlingly blue in the firelight. Slowly she drew her hands away from him, still looking straight into his eyes, and then she placed them against each of his arms and slowly lifted her face to him. Reverently he bent and kissed her.

"God bless you!" he whispered.

For hours after that he sat beside the fire. The wind came up stronger across the Barren; the storm broke fresh from the north, the spruce and the balsam wailed over his head, and he could hear the moaning sweep of the blizzard out in the open spaces. But the sounds came to him now like a new kind of music, and his heart throbbed and his soul was warm with joy as he looked at the little tent wherein there lay sleeping the woman whom he loved.

He still felt the warmth of her lips, he saw again and again the blue softness that had come for an instant into her eyes, and he thanked God for the wonderful happiness that had come to him. For the sweetness of the woman's lips and the greater sweetness of her blue eyes told him what life held for him now. A day's journey to the south was an Indian camp. He would take her there, and would hire runners to carry up Pelliter's medicines and his letters. Then he would go on-- with the woman-- and he laughed softly and joyously at the glorious news which he would take back to Pelliter a little later. For the kiss burned on his lips, the blue eyes smiled at him still from out of the firelit gloom, and he knew nothing but hope.

It was late, almost midnight, when he went to bed. With the storm wailing and twisting more fiercely about him, he fell asleep. And it was late when he awoke. The forest was filled with a moaning sound. The fire was low. Beyond it the flap of the woman's tent was still down, and he put on fresh fuel quietly, so that he would not awaken her. He looked at his watch and found that he had been sleeping for nearly seven hours. Then he returned to his tent to get the things for breakfast. Half a dozen paces from the door flap he stopped in sudden astonishment.

Hanging to his tent in the form of a great wreath was the red bakneesh which he had cut the night before, and over it, scrawled in charcoal on the silk, there stared at him the crudely written words:

"In honor of the living."

With a low cry he sprang back toward the other tent, and then, as sudden as his movement, there flashed upon him the significance of the bakneesh wreath. The woman was saying to him what she had not spoken in words. She had come out in the night while he was asleep and had hung the wreath where he would see it in the morning. The blood rushed warm and joyous through his body, and with something which was not a laugh, but which was an exultant breath from the soul itself, he straightened himself, and his hand fell in its old trick to his revolver holster. It was empty.

He dragged out his blankets, but the weapon was not between them. He looked into the corner where he had placed his rifle. That, too, was gone. His face grew tense and white as he walked slowly beyond the fire to the woman's tent. With his ear at the flap he listened. There was no sound within-- no sound of movement, of life, of a sleeper's breath; and like one who feared to reveal a terrible picture he drew back the flap. The balsam bed which he had made for the woman was empty, and across it had been drawn the big rough box. He stepped inside. The box was open-- and empty, except for a mass of worn and hard-packed balsam boughs in the bottom. In another instant the truth burst in all its force upon MacVeigh. The box had held life, and the woman--

Something on the side of the box caught his eyes. It was a folded bit of paper, pinned where he must see it. He tore it off and staggered with it back into the light of day. A low, hard cry came from his lips as he read what the woman had written to him:

> "May God bless you for being good to me. In the storm me have
> gone-- my husband and I. Word came to us that you were on our
> trail, and we saw your fire out on the Barren. My husband made the
> box for me to keep me from cold and storm. When we saw you we
> changed places, and so you met me with my dead. He could have
> killed you-- a dozen times, but you were good to me, and so you
> live. Some day may God give you a good woman who will love you as I
> love him. He killed a man, but killing is not always murder. We

have taken your weapons, and the storm will cover our trail. But you would not follow. I know that. For you know what it means to love a woman, and so you know what life means to a woman when she loves a man.   MRS. ISOBEL DEANE."

IV
THE MAN-HUNTERS

Like one dazed by a blow Billy read once more the words which Isobel Deane had left for him. He made no sound after that first cry that had broken from his lips, but stood looking into the crackling flames of the fire until a sudden lash of the wind whipped the note from between his fingers and sent it scurrying away in a white volley of fine snow. The loss of the note awoke him to action. He started to pursue the bit of paper, then stopped and laughed. It was a short, mirthless laugh, the kind of a laugh with which a strong man covers pain. He returned to the tent again and looked in. He flung back the tent flaps so that the light could enter and he could see into the box. A few hours before that box had hidden Scottie Deane, the murderer. And she was his wife ! He turned back to the fire, and he saw again the red bakneesh hanging over his tent flap, and the words she had scrawled with the end of a charred stick, "In honor of the living." That meant him. Something thick and uncomfortable rose in his throat, and a blur that was not caused by snow or wind filled his eyes. She had made a magnificent fight. And she had won. And it suddenly occurred to him that what she had said in the note was true, and that Scottie Deane could easily have killed him. The next moment he wondered why he had not done that. Deane had taken a big chance in allowing him to live. They had only a few hours' start of him, and their trail could not be entirely obliterated by the storm. Deane would be hampered in his flight by the presence of his wife. He could still follow and overtake them. They had taken his weapons, but this would not be the first time that he had gone after his man without weapons.

Swiftly the reaction worked in him. He ran beyond the fire, and circled quickly until he came upon the trail of the outgoing sledge. It was still quite distinct. Deeper in the forest it could be easily followed. Something fluttered at his feet. It was Isobel Deane's note. He picked it up, and again his eyes fell upon those last words that she had written: But you would not follow. I know that. For you know what it means to love a woman, and so you know what life means to a woman when she loves a man. That was why Scottie Deane had not killed him. It was because of the woman. And she had faith in him! This time he folded the note and placed it in his pocket, where the blue flower had been. Then he went slowly back to the fire.

"I told you I'd give him back his life-- if I could," he said. "And I guess I'm going to keep my word." He fell into his old habit of talking to himself-- a habit that comes easily to one in the big open spaces-- and he laughed as he stood beside the fire and loaded his pipe. "If it wasn't for her!" he added, thinking of Scottie Deane. "Gawd-- if it wasn't for her!"

He finished loading his pipe, and lighted it, staring off into the thicker spruce forest into which Scottie and his wife had fled. The entire force was on the lookout for Scottie Deane. For more than a year he had been as elusive as the little white ermine of the woods. He had outwitted the best men in the service, and his name was known to every man of the Royal Mounted from Calgary to Herschel Island. There was a price on his head, and fame for the man who captured him. Those who dreamed of promotions also dreamed of Scottie Deane; and as Billy thought of these things something that was not the man-hunting instinct rose in him and his blood warmed with a strange feeling of brotherhood. Scottie Deane was more than an outlaw to him now, more than a mere man. Hunted like a rat, chased from place to place, he must be more than those things for a woman like Isobel Deane still to cling to. He recalled the gentleness of her voice, the sweetness of her face, the tenderness of her blue eyes, and for the first time the thought came to him that such a woman could not love a man who was wholly bad. And she did love him. A twinge of pain came with that truth, and yet with it a thrill of pleasure. Her loyalty was a triumph-- even for him. She had come to him like an angel out of the storm, and she had gone from him like an angel. He was glad. A living, breathing reality had taken the place of the dream vision in his heart, a woman who was flesh and blood, and who was as true and as beautiful as the blue flower he had carried against his breast. In that moment he would have liked to grip Scottie Deane by the hand, because he was her husband and because he was man enough to make her love him.

Perhaps it was Deane who had hung the wreath of bakneesh on his tent and who had scribbled the words in charcoal. And Deane surely knew of the note his wife had written. The feeling of brotherhood grew stronger in Billy, and thought of their faith in him filled him with a strange elation.

The fire was growing low, and he turned to add fresh fuel. His eyes caught sight of the box in the tent, and he dragged it out. He was about to throw it on the fire when he hesitated and examined it more closely. How far had they come, he wondered? It must have been from the other side of the Barren, for Deane had built the box to protect Isobel from the fierce winds of the open. It was built of light, dry wood, hewn with a belt ax, and the corners were fastened with babiche cord made of caribou skin in place of nails. The balsam that had been placed in it for Isobel was still in the box, and Billy's heart beat a little more quickly as he drew it out. It had been Isobel's bed. He could see where the balsam was thicker, where her head had rested. With a sudden breathless cry he thrust the box on the fire.

He was not hungry, but he made himself a pot of coffee and drank it. Until now he had not observed that the storm was growing steadily worse. The thick, low-hanging spruce broke the force of it. Beyond the shelter of the forest he could hear the roar of it as it swept through the thin scrub and open spaces of the edge of the Barren. It recalled him once more to Pelliter. In the excitement of Isobel's presence and the shock and despair that had followed her flight he had been guilty of partly forgetting Pelliter. By the time he reached the Eskimo igloos there would be two days lost. Those two days might mean everything to his sick comrade. He jumped to his feet, felt in his pocket to see that the letters were safe, and began to arrange his pack. Through the trees there came now fine white volleys of blistering snow. It was like the hardest granulated sugar. A sudden blast of it stung his eyes; and, leaving his pack and tent, he made his way anxiously toward the more open timber and scrub. A few hundred yards from the camp he was forced to bow his head against the snow volleys and pull the broad flaps of his cap down over his cheeks and ears. A hundred yards more and he stopped, sheltering himself behind a gnarled and stunted banskian. He looked out into the beginning of the open. It was a white and seething chaos into which he could not see the distance of a pistol shot. The Eskimo igloos were twenty miles across the Barren, and Billy's heart sank. He could not make it. No man could live in the storm that was sweeping straight down from the Arctic, and he turned back to the camp. He had scarcely made the move when he was startled by a strange sound coming with the wind. He faced the white blur again, a hand dropping to his empty pistol holster. It came again, and this time he recognized it. It was a shout, a man's voice. Instantly his mind leaped to Deane and Isobel. What miracle could be bringing them back?

A shadow grew out of the twisting blur of the storm. It quickly separated itself into definite parts-- a team of dogs, a sledge, three men. A minute more and the dogs stopped in a snarling tangle as they saw Billy. Billy stepped forth. Almost instantly he found a revolver leveled at his breast.

"Put that up, Bucky Smith," he called. "If you're looking for a man you've found the wrong one!"

The man advanced. His eyes were red and staring. His pistol arm dropped as he came within a yard of Billy.

"By-- It's you, is it, Billy MacVeigh!" he exclaimed. His laugh was harsh and unpleasant. Bucky was a corporal in the service, and when Billy had last heard of him he was stationed at Nelson House. For a year the two men had been in the same patrol, and there was bad blood between them. Billy had never told of a certain affair down at Norway House, the knowledge of which at headquarters would have meant Bucky's disgraceful retirement from the force. But he had called Bucky out in fair fight and had whipped him within an inch of his life. The old hatred burned in the corporal's eyes as he stared into Billy's face. Billy ignored the look, and shook hands with the other men. One of them was a Hudson's Bay Company's driver, and the other was Constable Walker, from Churchill.

"Thought we'd never live to reach shelter," gasped Walker, as they shook hands. "We're out after Scottie Deane, and we ain't losing a minute. We're going to get him, too. His trail is so hot we can smell it. My God, but I'm bushed!"

The dogs, with the company man at their head, were already making for the camp. Billy grinned at the corporal as they followed.

"Had a pretty good chance to get me, if you'd been alone, didn't you, Bucky?" he asked, in a voice that Walker did not hear. "You see, I haven't forgotten your threat."

There was a steely hardness behind his laugh. He knew that Bucky Smith was a scoundrel whose good fortune was that he had never been found out in some of his evil work. In a flash his mind traveled back to that day at Norway House when Rousseau, the half Frenchman, had come to him from a sick-bed to tell him that Bucky had ruined his young wife. Rousseau, who should have been in bed with his fever, died two days later. Billy could still hear the taunt in Bucky's voice when he had cornered him with Rousseau's accusation, and the fight had followed. The thought that this man was now close after Isobel and Deane filled him with a sort of rage, and as Walker went ahead he laid a hand on Bucky's arm.

"I've been thinking about you of late, Bucky," he said. "I've been thinking a lot about that affair down at Norway, an' I've been lacking myself for not reporting it. I'm going to do it-- unless you cut a right-angle track to the one you're taking. I'm after Scottie Deane myself!"

In the next breath he could have cut out his tongue for having uttered the words. A gleam of triumph shot into Bucky's eyes.

"I thought we was right," he said. "We sort of lost the trail in the storm. Glad we found you to set us right. How much of a start of us has he and that squaw that's traveling with him got ?"

Billy's mittened hands clenched fiercely. He made no reply, but followed quickly after Walker. His mind worked swiftly. As he came in to the fire he saw that the dogs had already dropped down in their traces and that they were exhausted. Walker's face was pinched, his eyes half closed by the sting of the snow. The driver was half stretched out on the sledge, his feet to the fire. In a glance he had assured himself that both dogs and men had gone through a long and desperate struggle in the storm. He looked at Bucky, and this time there was neither rancor nor threat in his voice when he spoke.

"You fellows have had a hard time of it," he said. "Make yourselves at home. I'm not overburdened with grub, but if you'll dig out some of your own rations I'll get it ready while you thaw out."

Bucky was looking curiously at the two tents.

"Who's with you?" he asked.

Billy shrugged his shoulders. His voice was almost affable.

"Hate to tell you who was with me, Bucky," he laughed, "I came in late last night, half dead, and found a half-breed camped here-- in that silk tent. He was quite chummy-- mighty fine chap. Young fellow, too-- almost a kid. When I got up this morning--" Billy shrugged his shoulders again and pointed to his empty pistol holster. "Everything was gone-- dogs, sledge, extra tent, even my rifle and automatic. He wasn't quite bad, though, for he left me my grub. He was a funny cuss, too. Look at that!" He pointed to the bakneesh wreath that still hung to the front of his tent. "`In honor of the living,' " he read, aloud, "Just a sort of reminder, you know, that he might have hit me on the head with a club if he'd wanted to." He came nearer to Bucky, and said, good-naturedly: "I guess you've got me beat this time, Bucky. Scottie Deane is pretty safe from me, wherever he is. I haven't even got a gun!"

"He must have left a trail," remarked Bucky, eying him shrewdly.

"He did-- out there!"

As Bucky went to examine what was left of the trail Billy thanked Heaven that Deane had placed Isobel on the sledge before he left camp. There was nothing to betray her presence. Walker had unlaced their outfit, and Billy was busy preparing a meal when Bucky returned. There was a sneer on his lips.

"Didn't know you was that easy," he said. "Wonder why he didn't take his tent! Pretty good tent, isn't it?"

He went inside. A minute later he appeared at the flap and called to Billy.

"Look here!" he said, and there was a tremble of excitement in his voice. His eyes were blazing with an ugly triumph. "Your half-breed had pretty long hair, didn't he?"

He pointed to a splinter on one of the light tent-poles. Billy's heart gave a sudden jump. A tress of Isobel's long, loose hair had caught in the splinter, and a dozen golden-brown strands had remained to give him away. For a moment he forgot that Bucky Smith was watching him. He saw Isobel again as she had last entered the tent, her beautiful hair flowing in a firelit glory about her, her eyes still filled with tender gratitude. Once more he felt the warmth of her lips, the touch of her hand, the thrill of her presence near him. Perhaps these emotions covered any suspicious movement or word by which he might otherwise have betrayed himself. By the time they were gone he had recovered himself, and he turned to his companion with a low laugh.

"It's a woman's hair, all right, Bucky. He told me all sorts of nice things about a girl `back home.' They must have been true."

The eyes of the two men met unflinchingly. There was a sneer on Buck's lips; Billy was smiling.

"I'm going to follow this Frenchman after we've had a little rest," said the corporal, trying to cover a certain note of excitement and triumph in his voice. "There's a woman traveling with Scottie Deane, you know-- a white woman-- and there's only one other north of Churchill. Of course, you're anxious to get back your stolen outfit?"

"You bet I am," exclaimed Billy, concealing the effect of the bull's-eye shot Bucky had made. "I'm not particularly happy in the thought of reporting myself stripped in this sort of way. The breed will hang to thick cover, and it won't be difficult to follow his trail."

He saw that Bucky was a little taken aback by his ready acquiescence, and before the other could reply he hurried out to join Walker in the preparation of breakfast. He made a gallon of tea, fried some bacon, and brought out and toasted his own stock of frozen bannock. He made a second kettle of tea while the others were eating, and shook out the blankets in his own tent. Walker had told him that they had traveled nearly all night.

"Better have an hour or two of sleep before you go on," he invited.

The driver's name was Conway. He was the first to accept Billy's invitation. When he had finished eating, Walker followed him into the tent. When they were gone Bucky looked hard at Billy.

"What's your game?" he asked.

"The Golden Rule, that's all," replied Billy, proffering his tobacco. "The half-breed treated me square and made me comfortable, even if he did take his pay afterward. I'm doing the same."

"And what do you expect to take-- afterward?"

Billy's eyes narrowed as he returned the other's searching look.

"Bucky, I didn't think you were quite a fool," he said. "You've got a little decency in your hide, haven't you? A man might as well be in jail as up here without a gun. I expect you to contribute one-- when you go after the half-breed-- you or Walker. He'll do it if you won't. Better go in with the others. I'll keep up the fire."

Bucky rose sullenly. He was still suspicious of Billy's hospitality, but at the same time he could see the strength of Billy's argument and the importance of the price he was asking. He joined Walker and Conway. Fifteen minutes later Billy approached the tent and looked in. The three men were in the deep sleep of exhaustion. Instantly Billy's actions changed. He had thrown his pack outside the tent to make more room, and he quickly slipped a spare blanket in with his provisions. Then he entered the other tent, and a flush spread over his face, and he felt his blood grow warmer.

"You may be a fool, Billy MacVeigh," he laughed, softly. "You may be a fool, but we're going to do it!"

Gently he disentangled the long silken strands of golden brown from the tent-pole. He wound the hair about his fingers, and it made a soft and shining ring. It was all that he would ever possess of Isobel Deane, and his breath came more quickly as he pressed it for a moment to his rough and storm-beaten face. He put it in his pocket, carefully wrapped in Isobel's note, and then once more he went back to the tent in which the three men were sleeping. They had not moved. Walker's holster was within reach of his hand. For a moment the temptation to reach out and pluck the gun from it was strong. He pulled himself away. He would win in this fight with Bucky as surely as he had won in the other, and he would win without theft. Quickly he threw his pack over his shoulder and struck the trail made by Deane in his flight. On his snow-shoes he followed it in a long, swift pace. A hundred yards from the camp he looked back for an instant. Then he turned, and his face was grim and set.

"If you've got to be caught, it's not going to be by that outfit back there, Mr. Scottie Deane," he said to himself. "It's up to yours truly, and Billy MacVeigh is the man who can do the trick, if he hasn't got a gun!"

V

BILLY FOLLOWS ISOBEL

From the first Billy could see the difficulty with which Deane and his dogs had made their way through the soft drifts of snow piled up by the blizzard. In places where the trees had thinned out Deane had floundered ahead and pulled with the team. Only once in the first mile had Isobel climbed from the sledge, and that was where traces, toboggan, and team had all become mixed up in the snow-covered top of a fallen tree. The fact that Deane was compelling his wife to ride added to Billy's liking for the man. It was probable that Isobel had not gone to sleep at all after her hard experience on the Barren, but had lain awake planning with her husband until the hour of their flight. If Isobel had been able to travel on snow-shoes Billy reasoned that Deane would have left the dogs behind, for in the deep, soft snow he could have made better time without them, and snow-shoe trails would have been obliterated by the storm hours ago. As it was, he could not lose them. He knew that he had no time to lose if he made sure of beating out Bucky and his men. The suspicious corporal would not sleep long. While he had the advantage of being comparatively fresh, Billy's snow-shoes were smoothing and packing the trail, and the others, if they followed, would be able to travel a mile or two an hour faster than himself. That Bucky would follow he did not doubt for a moment. The corporal was already half convinced that Scottie Deane had made the trail from camp and that the hair he had found entangled in the splinter on the tent-pole belonged to the outlaw's wife. And Scottie Deane was too big a prize to lose.

Billy's mind worked rapidly as he bent more determinedly to the pursuit. He knew that there were only two things that Bucky could do under the circumstances. Either he would follow after him with Walker and the driver or he would come alone. If Walker and Conway accompanied him the fight for Scottie Deane's capture would be a fair one, and the man who first put manacles about the outlaw's wrists would be the victor. But if he left his two companions in camp and came after him alone--

The thought was not a pleasant one. He was almost sorry that he had not taken Walker's gun. If Bucky came alone it would be with but one purpose in mind-- to make sure of Scottie Dean by "squaring up" with him first. Billy was sure that he had measured the man right, and that he would not hesitate to carry out his old threat by putting a bullet into him at the first opportunity. And here would be opportunity. The storm would cover up any foul work he might accomplish, and his reward would be Scottie Deane-- unless Deane played too good a hand for him.

At thought of Deane Billy chuckled. Until now he had not taken him fully into consideration, and suddenly it dawned upon him that there was a bit of humor as well as tragedy in the situation. He cheerfully conceded to himself that for a long time Deane had proved himself a better man than either Bucky or himself, and that, after all, he was the man who held the situation well in hand even now. He was well armed. He was as cautions as a fox, and would not be caught napping. And yet this thought filled Billy with satisfaction rather than fear. Deane would be more than a match for Bucky alone if he failed in beating out the corporal. But if he did beat him out--

Billy's lips set grimly, and there was a hard light in his eyes as he glanced back over his shoulder. He would not only beat him out, but he would capture Scottie Deane. It would be a game of fox against fox, and he would win. No one would ever know why he was playing the game as he had planned to play it. Bucky would never know. Down at headquarters they would never know. And yet deep down in his heart he hoped and believed that Isobel would guess and understand. To save Deane, to save Isobel, he must keep them out of the hands of Bucky Smith, and to do that he must make them his own prisoners. It would be a terrible ordeal at first. A picture of Isobel rose before him, her faith and trust in him broken, her face white and drawn with grief and despair, her blue eyes flashing at him-- hatred. But he felt now that he could stand those things. One moment-- the fatal moment, when she would understand and know that he had remained true-- would repay him for what he might suffer.

He traveled swiftly for an hour, and paused then to get his wind where the partly covered trail dipped down into a frozen swamp. Here Isobel had climbed from the sledge and had followed in the path of the toboggan. In places where the spruce and balsam were thick overhead Billy could make out the imprints of her moccasins. Deane had led the dogs in the darkness of the storm, and twice Billy found the burned ends of matches, where he had stopped to look at his compass. He was striking a course almost due west. At the farther edge of the swamp the trail struck a lake, and straight across this Deane had led his team. The worst of the storm was over now. The wind was slowly shifting to the south and east, and the fine, steely snow had given place to a thicker and softer downfall. Billy shuddered as he thought of what this lake must have been a few hours before, when Isobel and Deane had crossed it in the thick blackness of the blizzard that had swept it like a hurricane.

It was half a mile across the lake, and here, fifty yards from shore, the trail was completely covered. Billy lost no time by endeavoring to find signs of it in the open, but struck directly for the opposite timber field and swung along in the shelter of the scrub forest. He picked up the trail easily. Half an hour later he stopped. Spruce and balsam grew thick about him, shutting out what was left of the wind. Here Scottie Deane had stopped to build a fire. Close to the charred embers was a mass of balsam boughs on which Isobel had rested. Scottie had made a pot of boiling tea and had afterward thrown the grounds on the snow. The warm bodies of the dogs had made smooth, round pits in the snow, and Billy figured that the fugitives had rested for a couple of hours. They had traveled eight miles through the blizzard without a fire, and his heart was filled with a sickening pain as he thought of Isobel Deane and the suffering he had brought to her. For a few moments there swept over him a revulsion for that thing which he stood for-- the Law. More than once in his experience he had thought that its punishment had been greater than the crime. Isobel had suffered, and was suffering, far more than if Deane had been captured a year before and hanged. And Deane himself had paid a penalty greater than death in being a witness of the suffering of the woman who had remained loyal to him. Billy's heart went out to them in a low, yearning cry as he looked at the balsam bed and the black char of the fire. He wished that he could give them, life and freedom and happiness, and his hands clenched tightly as he thought that he was willing to surrender everything, even to his own honor, for the woman he loved.

Fifteen minutes after he had struck the shelter of the camp he was again in pursuit. His blood leaped a little excitedly when he found that Scottie Deane's trail was now almost as straight as a plumb-line and that the sledge no longer became entangled in hidden windfalls and brush. It was proof that it was light when Deane and Isobel had left their camp. Isobel was walking now, and their sledge was traveling faster. Billy encouraged his own pace, and over two or three open spaces he broke into a long, swinging run. The trail was comparatively fresh, and at the end of another hour he knew that they could not be far ahead of him. He had followed through a thin swamp and had climbed to the top of a rough ridge when he stopped. Isobel had reached the bald cap of the ridge exhausted. The last twenty yards he could see where Deane had assisted her; and then she had dropped down in the snow, and he had placed a blanket under her. They had taken a drink of tea made back over the fire, and a little of it had fallen into the snow. It had not yet formed ice, and instinctively he dropped behind a rock and looked down into the wooded valley at his feet. In a few moments he began to descend.

He had almost reached the foot of the ridge when he brought himself short with a sudden low cry of horror. He had reached a point where the side of the ridge seemed to have broken off, leaving a precipitous wall. In a flash he realized what had happened. Deane and Isobel had descended upon a "snow trap," and it had given way under their weight, plunging them to the rocks below. For no longer than a breath he stood still, and in that moment there came a sound from far behind that sent a strange thrill through him. It was the howl of a dog. Bucky and his men were in close pursuit, and they were traveling with the team.

He swung a little to the left to escape the edge of the trap and plunged recklessly to the bottom. Not until he saw where Scottie Deane and the team had dragged themselves from the snow avalanche did he breathe freely again. Isobel was safe! He laughed in his joy and wiped the nervous sweat from his face as he saw the prints of her moccasins where Deane had righted the sledge. And then, for the first time, he observed a number of small red stains on the snow. Either Isobel or Deane had been injured in the fall, perhaps slightly. A hundred yards from the "trap" the sledge had stopped again, and from this point it was Deane who rode and Isobel who walked!

He followed more cautiously now. Another hundred yards and he stopped to sniff the air. Ahead of him the spruce and balsam grew close and thick, and from that shelter he was sure that something was coming to him on the air. At first he thought it was the odor of the balsam. A moment later he knew that it was smoke.

Force of habit brought his hand for the twentieth time to his empty pistol holster. Its emptiness added to the caution with which he approached the thick spruce and balsam ahead of him. Taking advantage of a mass of low snow-laden bushes, he swung out at a right angle to the trail and began making a wide circle. He worked swiftly. Within half or three-quarters of an hour Bucky would reach the ridge. Whatever he accomplished must be done before then. Five minutes after leaving the trail he caught his first glimpse of smoke and began to edge in toward the fire. The stillness oppressed him. He drew nearer and nearer, yet he heard no sound of voice or of the dogs. At last he reached a point where he could look out from behind a young ground spruce and see the fire. It was not more than thirty feet away. He held his breath tensely at what he saw. On a blanket spread out close to the fire lay Scottie Deane, his head pillowed on a pack-sack. There was no sign of Isobel, and no sign of the sledge and dogs. Billy's heart thumped excitedly as he rose to his feet. He did not stop to ask himself where Isobel and the dogs had gone. Deane was alone, and lay with his back toward him. Fate could not have given him a better opportunity, and his moccasined feet fell swiftly and quietly in the snow. He was within six feet of Scottie before the injured man heard him, and scarcely had the other moved when he was upon him. He was astonished at the ease with which he twisted Deane upon his back and put the handcuffs about his wrists. The work was no sooner done than he understood. A rag was tied about Deane's head, and it was stained with blood. The man's arms and body were limp. He looked at Billy with dulled eyes, and as he slowly realized what had happened a groan broke from his lips.

In an instant Billy was on his knees beside him. He had seen Deane twice before, over at Churchill, but this was the first time that he had ever looked closely into his face. It was a face worn by hardship and mental torture. The cheeks were thinned, and the steel-gray eyes that looked up into Billy's were reddened by weeks and months of fighting against storm. It was the face, not of a criminal, but of a man whom Billy would have trusted-- blonde-mustached, fearless, and filled with that clean-cut strength which associates itself with fairness and open fighting. Hardly had he drawn a second breath when Billy realized why this man had not killed him when he had the chance. Deane was not of the sort to strike in the dark or from behind. He had let Billy live because he still believed in the manhood of man, and the thought that he had repaid Deane's faith in him by leaping upon him when he was down and wounded filled Billy with a bitter shame. He gripped one of Deane's hands in his own.

"I hate to do this, old man," he cried, quickly. "It's hell to put those things on a man who's hurt. But I've got to do it. I didn't mean to come-- no, s'elp me God, I didn't-- if Bucky Smith and two others hadn't hit your trail back at the old camp. They'd have got you-- sure. And she wouldn't have been safe with them. Understand ? She wouldn't have been safe! So I made up my mind to beat on ahead and take you myself. I want you to understand. And you do know, I guess. You must have heard, for I thought you were sure-enough dead in the box, an' I swear to Heaven I meant all I said then. I wouldn't have come. I was glad you two got away. But this Bucky is a skunk and a scoundrel-- and mebbe if I take you-- I can help you-- later on. They'll be here in a few minutes."

He spoke quickly, his voice quivering with the emotion that inspired his words, and not for an instant did Scottie Deane allow his eyes to shift from Billy's face. When Billy stopped he still looked at him for a moment, judging the truth of what he had heard by what he saw in the other's face. And then Billy felt his hand tighten for an instant about his own.

"I guess you're pretty square, MacVeigh," he said, "and I guess it had to come pretty soon, too. I'm not sorry that it's you-- and I know you'll take care of her."

"I'll do it-- if I have to fight-- and kill!"

Billy had withdrawn his hand, and both were clenched. Into Deane's eyes there leaped a sudden flash of fire.

"That's what I did," he breathed, gripping his fingers hard. "I killed-- for her. He was a skunk-- and a scoundrel-- too. And you'd have done it!" He looked at Billy again. "I'm glad you said what you did-- when I was in the box," he added. "If she wasn't as pure and as sweet as the stars I'd feel different. But it's just sort of in my bones that you'll treat her like a brother. I haven't had faith in many men. I've got it in you."

Billy leaned low over the other. His face was flushed, and his voice trembled.

"God bless you for that, Scottie!" he said.

A sound from the forest turned both men's eyes.

"She took the dogs and went out there a little way for a load of wood," said Deane. "She's coming back."

Billy had leaped to his feet, and turned his face toward the ridge. He, too, had heard a sound-- another sound, and from another direction. He laughed grimly as he turned to Deane.

"And they're coming, too, Scottie," he replied. "They're climbing the ridge. I'll take your guns, old man. It's just possible there may be a fight!"

He slipped Deane's revolver into his holster and quickly emptied the chamber of the rifle that stood near.

"Where's mine?" he asked.

"Threw 'em away," said Deane. "Those are the only guns in the outfit."

Billy waited while Isobel Deane came through low-hanging spruce with the dogs.

VI
THE FIGHT

There was a smile for Deane on Isobel's lips as she struggled through the spruce, knee-deep in snow, the dogs tugging at the sledge behind her. And then in a moment she saw MacVeigh, and the smile froze into a look of horror on her face. She was not twenty feet distant when she emerged into the little opening, and Billy heard the rattling cry in her throat. She stopped, and her hands went to her breast. Deane had half raised himself, his pale, thin face smiling encouragingly at her; and with a wild cry Isobel rushed to him and flung herself upon her knees at his side, her hands gripping fiercely at the steel bands about his wrists. Billy turned away. He could hear her sobbing, and he could hear the low, comforting voice of the injured man. A groan of anguish rose to his own lips, and he clenched his hands hard, dreading the terrible moment when he would have to face the woman he loved above all else on earth.

It was her voice that brought him about. She had risen to her feet, and she stood before him panting like a hunted animal, and Billy saw in her face the thing which he had feared more than the sting of death. No longer were her blue eyes filled with the sweetness and faith of the angel who had come to him from out of the Barren. They were hard and terrible and filled with that madness which made him think she was about to leap upon him. In those eyes, in the quivering of her bare throat, in the sobbing rise and fall of her breast were the rage, the grief, and the fear of one whose faith had turned suddenly into the deadliest of all emotions; and Billy stood before her without a word on his lips, his face as cold and as bloodless as the snow under his feet.

"And so you-- you followed-- after-- that!"

It was all she said, and yet the voice, the significance of the choking words, hurt him more than if she had struck him. In them there was none of the passion and condemnation he had expected. Quietly, almost whisperingly uttered, they stung him to the soul. He had meant to say to her what he had said to Deane-- even more. But the crudeness of the wilderness had made him slow of tongue, and while his heart cried out for words Isobel turned and went to her husband. And then there came the thing he had been expecting. Down the ridge there raced a flurry of snow and a yelping of dogs. He loosened the revolver in his holster, and stood in readiness when Bucky Smith ran a few paces ahead of his men into the camp. At sight of his enemy's face, torn between rage and disappointment, all of Billy's old coolness returned to him.

With a bound Bucky was at Scottie Deane's side. He looked down at his manacled hands and at the woman who was clasping them in her own, and then he whirled on Billy with the quickness of a cat.

"You're a liar and a sneak!" he panted. "You'll answer for this at headquarters. I understand now why you let 'em go back there. It was her! She paid you-- paid you in her own way-- to free him! But she won't pay you again--"

At his words Deane had started as if stung by a wasp. Billy saw Isobel's whitened face. The meaning of Buck's words had gone home to her as swiftly as a lightning flash, and for an instant her eyes had turned to him! Bucky got no further than those last words. Before he could add another syllable Billy was upon him. His fist shot out-- once, twice-- and the blows that fell sent Bucky crashing through the fire. Billy did not wait for him to regain his feet. A red light blazed before his eyes. He forgot the presence of Deane and Walker and Conway. His one thought was that the scoundrel he had struck down had flung at Isobel the deadliest insult that a man could offer a woman, and before either Conway or Walker could make a move he was upon Bucky. He did not know how long or how many times he struck, but when at last Conway and Walker succeeded in dragging him away Bucky lay upon his back in the snow, blood gushing from his mouth and nose. Walker ran to him. Panting for breath, Billy turned toward Isobel and Deane. He was almost sobbing. He made no effort to speak. But he saw that the thing he had dreaded was gone. Isobel was looking at him again-- and there was the old faith in her eyes. At last-- she understood! Dean's handcuffed hands were clenched. The light of brotherhood shone in his eyes, and where a moment before there had been grief and despair in Billy's heart there came now a warm glow of joy. Once more they had faith in him!

Walker had raised Bucky to a sitting posture, and was wiping the blood from his face when Billy went to them. The corporal's hand made a limp move toward his revolver. Billy struck it away and secured the weapon. Then he spoke to Walker.

"There is no doubt in your mind that I hold a sergeancy in the service, is there, Walker?" he asked.

His tone was no longer one of comradeship. In it there was the ring of authority. Walker was quick to understand.

"None, sir!"

"And you are familiar with our laws governing insubordination and conduct unbecoming an officer of the service?"

Walker nodded.

"Then, as a superior officer and in the name of his Majesty the King, I place Corporal Bucky Smith under arrest, and commission you, under oath of the service, to take him under your guard to Churchill, along with the letter which I shall give you for the officer in charge there. I shall appear against him a little later with the evidence that will outlaw him from the service. Put the handcuffs on him!"

Stunned by the sudden change in the situation, Walker obeyed without a word. Billy turned to Conway, the driver.

"Deane is too badly injured to travel," he explained, " Put up your tent for him and his wife close to the fire. You can take mine in exchange for it as you go back."

He went to his kit and found a pencil and paper. Fifteen minutes later he gave Walker the letter in which he described to the commanding officer at Churchill certain things which he knew would hold Bucky a prisoner until he could personally appear against him. Meanwhile Conway had put up the tent and had assisted Deane into it. Isobel had accompanied him. Billy then had a five-minute confidential talk with Walker, and when the constable gave instructions for Conway to prepare the dogs for the return trip there was a determined hardness in his eyes as he looked at Bucky. In those five minutes he had heard the story of Rousseau, the young Frenchman down at Norway House, and of the wife whose faithlessness had killed him. Besides, he hated Bucky Smith, as all men hated him. Billy was confident that he could rely upon him.

Not until dogs and sledge were ready did Bucky utter a word. The terrific beating he had received had stunned him for a few minutes; but now he jumped to his feet, not waiting for the command from Walker, and strode up close to Billy. There was a vengeful leer on his bloody face and his eyes blazed almost white, but his voice was so low that Conway and Walker could only hear the murmur of it. His words were meant for Billy alone.

"For this I'm going to kill you, MacVeigh," he said; and in spite of Billy's contempt for the man there was a quality in the low voice that sent a curious shiver through him. "You can send me from the service, but you're going to die for doing it!"

Billy made no reply, and Bucky did not wait for one. He set off at the head of the sledge, with Conway a step behind them. Billy followed with Walker until they reached the foot of the ridge. There they shook hands, and Billy stood watching them until they passed over the cap of the ridge.

He returned to the camp slowly. Deane had emerged from the tent, supported by Isobel. They waited for him, and in Deane's face he saw the look that had filled it after he had struck down Bucky Smith. For a moment he dared not look at Isobel. She saw the change in him, and her cheeks flushed. Deane would have extended his hands, but she was holding them tightly in her own.

"You'd better go into the tent and keep quiet," advised Billy. "I haven't had time yet to see if you're badly hurt."

"It's not bad," Deane assured him. "I bumped into a rock sliding down the ridge, and it made me sick for a few minutes."

Billy knew that Isobel's eyes were on him, and he could almost feel their questioning. He began to take wood from the sledge she had loaded and throw it on the fire. He wished that Scottie and she had remained in the tent for a little longer. His face burned and his blood seemed like fire when he caught a glimpse of the steel cuffs about Deane's wrists. Through the smoke he saw Isobel still clasping her husband. He could see one of her little hands gripping at the steel band, and suddenly he sprang across and faced them, no longer fearing to meet Isobel's eyes or Deane's. Now his face was aflame, and he half held out his arms to them as he spoke, as though he would clasp them both to him in this moment of sacrifice and self-abnegation and the dawning of new life.

"You know-- you both know why I've done this!" he cried, "You heard what I said back there, Deane-- when you was in the box; an' all I said was true. She came to me out of that storm like an angel-- an' I'll think of her as an angel all my life. I don't know much about God-- not the God they have down there, where they take an eye for an eye an' a tooth for a tooth and kill because some one else has killed. But there's something up here in the big open places, something that makes you think and makes you want to do what's right and square; an' she's got all I know of God in that little Bible of mine-- the blue flower. I gave the blue flower to her, an' now an' forever she's my blue flower. I ain't ashamed to tell you, Deane, because you've heard it before, an' you know I'm not thinking it in a sinful way. It 'll help me if I can see her face an' hear her voice and know there's such love as yours after you're gone. For I'm going to let you go, Deane, old man. That's what I came for, to save you from the others an' give you back to her. I guess mebbe you'll know-- now-- how I feel--"

His voice choked him. Isobel's glorious eyes were looking into his soul, and he looked straight back into them and saw all his reward there. He turned to Deane. His key clicked in the locks to the handcuffs, and as they fell into the snow the two men gripped hands, and in their strong faces was that rarest of all things-- love of man for man.

"I'm glad you know," said Billy, softly. "It wouldn't be fair if you didn't, Scottie. I can think of her now, an' it won't be mean and low. And if you ever need help-- if you're down in South America or Africa-- anywhere-- I'll come if you send word. You'd better go to South America. That's a good place. I'll report to headquarters that you died-- from the fall. It's a lie, but blue flower would do it, and so will I. Sometimes, you know, the friend who lies is the only friend who's true-- and she'd do it-- a thousand times-- for you."

"And for you," whispered Isobel.

She was holding out her hands, her blue eyes streaming with tears of happiness, and for a moment Billy accepted one of them and held it in his own. He looked over her head as she spoke.

"God will bless you for this-- some day," she said; and a sob broke in her voice. "He will bring you happiness-- happiness-- in what you have dreamed of. You will find a blue flower   sweet and pure and loyal   and then you will know, even more fully, what life means to me with him."

And then she broke down, sobbing like a child, and with her face buried in her hands turned into the tent.

"Gawd!" whispered Billy, drawing a deep breath.

He looked Deane in the eyes; and Deane smiled, a rare and beautiful smile.

For a quarter of an hour they talked alone, and then Billy drew a wallet from his pocket.

"You'll need money, Scottie," he said. "I don't want you to lose a minute in getting out of the country. Make for Vancouver. I've got three hundred dollars here. You've got to take it or I'll shoot you!"

He thrust the money into Deane's hands as Isobel came out of the tent. Her eyes were red, but she was smiling; and she held something in her hand. She showed it to the two men. It was the blue flower Billy had given her. But now its petals were torn apart, and nine of them lay in the palm of her hand.

"It can't go with one." She spoke softly and the smile died on her lips. "There are nine petals, three for each of us."

She gave three to her husband and three to Billy, and for a moment the men stared at them as they lay in their rough and calloused palms. Then Billy drew out the bit of buckskin in which he had placed the strands of Isobel's hair and slipped the blue petals in with them. Deane had drawn a worn envelope from his pocket. Billy spoke low to Deane.

"I want to be alone for a while-- until dinner-time. Will you go into the tent-- with her ?"

When they were gone Billy went to the spot where he had dropped his pack before crawling up on Deane. He picked it up and slipped it over his shoulders as he walked. He went swiftly back over his old trail, and this time it was with a heart leaden with a deep and terrible loneliness. When he reached the ridge he tried to whistle, but his lips seemed thick, and there was something in his throat that choked him. From the cap of the ridge he looked down. A thin mist of smoke was rising from out of the spruce. It blurred before his eyes, and a sobbing break came in his low cry of Isobel's name. Then he turned once more back into the loneliness and desolation of his old life.

"I'm coming, Pelly," he laughed, in a strained, hard way. "I haven't given you exactly a square deal, old man, but I'll hustle and make up for lost time!"

A wind was beginning to moan in the spruce tops again. He was glad of that. It promised storm. And a storm would cover up all trails.

VII
THE MADNESS OF PELLITER

Away up at Fullerton Point amid the storm and crash of the arctic gloom Pelliter fought himself through day after day of fever, waiting for MacVeigh. At first he had been filled with hope. That first glimpse of the sun they had seen through the little window on the morning that Billy left for Fort Churchill had come just in time to keep reason from snapping in his head. For three days after that he looked through the window at the same hour and prayed moaningly for another glimpse of that paradise in the southern sky. But the storm through which Isobel had struggled across the Barren gathered over his head and behind him, day after day of it, rolling and twisting and moaning with the roar of the cracking fields of ice, bringing back once more the thick death-gloom of the arctic night that had almost driven him mad. He tried to think only of Billy, of his loyal comrade's race into the south, and of the precious letters he would bring back to him; and he kept track of the days by making pencil marks on the door that opened out upon the gray and purple desolation of the arctic sea.

At last there came the day when he gave up hope. He believed that he was dying. He counted the marks on the door and found that there were sixteen. Just that many days ago Billy had set off with the dogs. If all had gone well he was a third of the way back, and within another week would be "home."

Pelliter's thin, fever-flushed face relaxed into a wan smile as he counted the pencil marks again. Long before that week was ended he figured that he would be dead. The medicines-- and the letters-- would come too late, probably four or five days too late. Straight out from his last mark he drew a long line, and at the end of it added in a scrawling, almost unintelligible, hand: "Dear Billy, I guess this is going to be my last day." Then he staggered from the door to the window.

Out there was what was killing him-- loneliness, a maddening desolation, a lifeless world that reached for hundreds of miles farther than his eyes could see. To the north and east there was nothing but ice, piled-up masses and grinning mountains of it, white at first, of a somber gray farther off, and then purple and almost black. There came to him now the low, never-ceasing thunder of the undercurrents fighting their way down from the Arctic Ocean, broken now and then by a growling roar as the giant forces sent a crack, like a great knife, through one of the frozen mountains. He had listened to those sounds for five months, and in those five months he had heard no other voice but his own and MacVeigh's and the babble of an Eskimo. Only once in four months had he seen the sun, and that was on the morning that MacVeigh went south. So he had gone half mad. Others had gone completely mad before him. Through the window his eyes rested on the five rough wooden crosses that marked their graves. In the service of the Royal Northwest Mounted Police they were called heroes. And in a short time he, Constable Pelliter, would be numbered among them. MacVeigh would send the whole story down to her, the true little girl a thousand miles south; and she would always remember him-- her hero-- and his lonely grave at Point Fullerton, the northernmost point of the Law. But she would never see that grave. She could never come to put flowers on it, as she put flowers on the grave of his mother; she would never know the whole story, not a half of it-- his terrible longing for a sound of her voice, a touch of her hand, a glimpse of her sweet blue eyes before he died. They were to be married in August, when his service in the Royal Mounted ended. She would be waiting for him. And in August-- or July-- word would reach her that he had died.

With a dry sob he turned from the window to the rough table that he had drawn close to his bunk, and for the thousandth time he held before his red and feverish eyes a photograph. It was a portrait of a girl, marvelously beautiful to Tommy Pelliter, with soft brown hair and eyes that seemed always to talk to him and tell him how much she loved him. And for the thousandth time he turned the picture over and read the words she had written on the back:

"My own dear boy, remember that I am always with you, always thinking of you, always praying for you; and I know, dear, that you will always do what you would do if I were at your side."

"Good Lord!" groaned Pelliter. "I can't die! I can't! I've got to live-- to see her--"

He dropped back on his bunk exhausted. The fires burned in his head again. He grew dizzy, and he talked to her, or thought he was talking, but it was only a babble of incoherent sound that made Kazan, the one-eyed old Eskimo dog, lift his shaggy head and sniff suspiciously. Kazan had listened to Pelliter's deliriums many times since MacVeigh had left them alone, and soon he dropped his muzzle between his forepaws and dozed again. A long time afterward he raised his head once more. Pelliter was quiet. But the dog sniffed, went to the door, whined softly, and nervously muzzled the sick man's thin hand. Then he settled back on his haunches, turned his nose straight up, and from his throat there came that wailing, mourning cry, long-drawn and terrible, with which Indian dogs lament before the tepees of masters who are newly dead. The sound aroused Pelliter. He sat up again, and he found that once more the fire and the pain had gone from his head.

"Kazan, Kazan," he pleaded, weakly, "it isn't time-- yet!"

Kazan had gone to the window that looked to the west, and stood with his forefeet on the sill. Pelliter shivered.

"Wolves again," he said, "or mebbe a fox."

He had grown into that habit of talking to himself, which is as common as human life itself in the far north, where one's own voice is often the one thing that breaks a killing monotony. He edged his way to the window as he spoke and looked out with Kazan. Westward there stretched the lifeless Barren illimitable and void, without rock or bush and overhung by a sky that always made Pelliter think of a terrible picture he had once seen of Doré's "Inferno." It was a low, thick sky, like purple and blue granite, always threatening to pitch itself down in terrific avalanches, and between the earth and this sky was the thin, smothered worldrM which MacVeigh had once called God's insane asylum.

Through the gloom Kazan's one eye and Pelliter's feverish vision could not see far, but at last the man made out an object toiling slowly toward the cabin. At first he thought it was a fox, and then a wolf, and then, as it loomed larger, a straying caribou. Kazan whined. The bristles along his spine rose stiff and menacing. Pelliter stared harder and harder, with his face pressed close against the cold glass of the window, and suddenly he gave a gasping cry of excitement. It was a man who was toiling toward the cabin! He was bent almost double, and he staggered in a zigzag fashion as he advanced. Pelliter made his way feebly to the door, unbarred it, and pushed it partly open. Overcome by weakness he fell back then on the edge of his bunk,

It seemed an age before he heard steps. They were slow and stumbling, and an instant later a face appeared at the door. It was a terrible face, overgrown with beard, with wild and staring eyes; but it was a white man's face. Pelliter had expected an Eskimo, and he sprang to his feet with sudden strength as the stranger came in.

"Something to eat, mate, for the love o' God give me something to eat!"

The stranger fell in a heap on the floor and stared up at him with the ravenous entreaty of an animal. Pelliter's first move was to get whisky, and the other drank it in great gulps. Then he dragged himself to his feet, and Pelliter sank in a chair beside the table.

"I'm sick," he said. "Sergeant MacVeigh has gone to Churchill, and I guess I'm in a bad way. You'll have to help yourself. There's meat-- 'n' bannock--"

Whisky had revived the new-comer. He stared at Pelliter, and as he stared he grinned, ugly yellow teeth leering from between his matted beard. The look cleared Pelliter's brain. For some reason which he could not explain, his pistol hand fell to the place where he usually carried his holster. Then he remembered that his service revolver was under the pillow.

"Fever," said the sailor; for Pelliter knew that he was a sailor.

He took off his heavy coat and tossed it on the table. Then he followed Pelliter's instructions in quest of food, and for ten minutes ate ravenously. Not until he was through and seated opposite him at the table did Pelliter speak.

"Who are you, and where in Heaven's name did you come from?" he asked.

"Blake-- Jim Blake's my name, an' I come from what I call Starvation Igloo Inlet, thirty miles up the coast. Five months ago I was left a hundred miles farther up to take care of a cache for the whaler John B. Sidney, and the cache was swept away by an overflow of ice. Then we struck south, hunting and starving, me 'n' the woman--"

"The woman!" cried Pelliter.

"Eskimo squaw," said Blake, producing a black pipe. "The cap'n bought her to keep me company-- paid four sacks of flour an' a knife to her husband up at Wagner

Inlet. Got any tobacco?"

Pelliter rose to get the tobacco. He was surprised to find that he was steadier on his feet and that Blake's words were clearing his brain. That had been his and MacVeigh's great fight-- the fight to put an end to the white man's immoral trade in Eskimo women and girls, and Blake had already confessed himself a criminal. Promise of action, quick action, momentarily overcame his sickness. He went back with the tobacco, and sat down.

"Where's the woman?" be asked.

"Back in the igloo," said Blake, filling his pipe. "We killed a walrus up there and built an icehouse. The meat's gone. She's probably gone by this time." He laughed coarsely across at Pelliter as he lighted his pipe. "It seems good to get into a white man's shack again."

"She's not dead?" insisted Pelliter.

"Will be-- shortly," replied Blake. "She was so weak she couldn't walk when I left. But them Eskimo animals die hard, 'specially the women."

"Of course you're going back for her?"

The other stared for a moment into Pelliter's flushed face, and then laughed as though he had just heard a good joke.

"Not on your life, my boy. I wouldn't hike that thirty miles again-- an' thirty back-- for all the Eskimo women up at Wagner."

The red in Pelliter's eyes grew redder as he leaned over the table.

"See here," he said, "you're going back-- now! Do you understand? You're go-ing back!"

Suddenly he stopped. He stared at Blake's coat, and with a swiftness that took the other by surprise he reached across and picked something from it. A startled cry broke from his lips. Between his fingers he held a single filament of hair. It was nearly a foot long, and it was not an Eskimo woman's hair. It shone a dull gold in the gray light that came through the window. He raised his eyes, terrible in their accusation of the man opposite him.

"You lie!" he said. "She's not an Eskimo!"

Blake had half risen, his great hands clutching the ends of the table, his brutal face thrust forward, his whole body in an attitude that sent Pelliter back out of his reach. He was not an instant too soon. With an oath Blake sent the table crashing aside and sprang upon the sick man.

"I'll kill you!" he cried. "I'll kill you, an' put you where I've put her, 'n' when your pard comes back I'll--"

His hands caught Pelliter by the throat, but not before there had come from between the sick man's lips a cry of "Kazan! Kazan!"

With a wolfish snarl the old one-eyed sledge-dog sprang upon Blake, and the three fell with a crash upon Pelliter's bunk. For an instant Kazan's attack drew one of Blake's powerful hands from Pelliter's throat, and as he turned to strike off the dog Pelliter's hand groped out under his flattened pillow. Blake's murderous face was still turned when he drew out his heavy service revolver; and as Blake cut at Kazan with a long sheath-knife which he had drawn from his belt Pelliter fired. Blake's grip relaxed. Without a groan he slipped to the floor, and Pelliter staggered back to his feet. Kazan's teeth were buried in Blake's leg.

"There, there, boy," said Pelliter, pulling him away. "That was a close one!"

He sat down and looked at Blake. He knew that the man was dead. Kazan was sniffing about the sailor's head with stiffened spines. And then a ray of light flashed for an instant through the window. It was the sun-- the second time that Pelliter had seen it in four months. A cry of joy welled up from his heart. But it was stopped midway. On the floor close beside Blake something glittered in the fiery ray, and Pelliter was upon his knees in an instant. It was the short golden hair he had snatched from the dead man's coat, and partly covering it was the picture of his sweetheart which had fallen when the table was overturned. With the photograph in one hand and that single thread of woman's hair between the fingers of his other Pelliter rose slowly to his feet and faced the window. The sun was gone. But its coming had put a new life into him. He turned joyously to Kazan.

"That means something, boy," he said, in a low, awed voice, "the sun, the picture, and this! She sent it, do you hear, boy? She sent it! I can almost hear her voice, an' she's telling me to go. 'Tommy,' she's saying, 'you wouldn't be a man if you didn't go, even though you know you're going to die on the way. You can take her something to eat,' she's saying, boy, 'an' you can just as well die in an igloo as here. You can leave word for Billy, an' you can take her grub enough to last until he comes, an' then he'll bring her down here, an' you'll be buried out there with the others just the same.' That's what she's saying, Kazan, so we're going!" He looked about him a little wildly. "Straight up the coast," he mumbled. "Thirty miles. We might make it."

He began filling a pack with food. Outside the door there was a small sledge, and after he had bundled himself in his traveling-clothes he dragged the pack to the sledge, and behind the pack tied on a bundle of firewood, a lantern, blankets, and oil. After he had done this he wrote a few lines to MacVeigh and pinned the paper to the door. Then he hitched old Kazan to the sledge and started off, leaving the dead man where he had fallen.

"It's what she'd have us do," he said again to Kazan. "She sure would have us do this, Kazan. God bless her dear little heart!"

VIII
LITTLE MYSTERY

Pelliter hung close to the ice-bound coast. He traveled slowly, leading the way for Kazan, who strained every muscle in his aged body to drag the sledge. For a time the excitement of what had occurred gave Pelliter a strength which soon began to ebb. But his old weakness did not entirely return. He found that his worst trouble at first was in his eyes. Weeks of fever had enfeebled his vision until the world about him looked new and strange. He could see only a few hundred paces ahead, and beyond this little circle everything turned gray and black. Singularly enough, it struck him that there was some humor as well as tragedy in the situation, that there was something to laugh at in the fact that Kazan had but one eye, and that he was nearly blind. He chuckled to himself and spoke aloud to the dog.

"Makes me think of the games o' hide-'n'-seek we used to play when we were kids, boy," he said. "She used to tie her handkerchief over my eyes, 'n' then I'd follow her all through the old orchard, and when I caught her it was a part of the game she'd have to let me kiss her. Once I bumped into an apple tree--"

The toe of his snow-shoe caught in an ice-hummock and sent him face downward into the snow. He picked himself up and went on.

"We played that game till we was grown-ups, old man," he went on. "Last time we played it she was seventeen. Had her hair in a big brown braid, an' it all came undone so that when I caught her an' took off the handkerchief I could just see her eyes an' her mouth laughing at me, and it was that time I hugged her up closer than ever and told her I was going out to make a home for us. Then I came up here."

He stopped and rubbed his eyes; and for an hour after that, as he plodded onward, he mumbled things which neither Kazan nor any other living thing could have understood. But whatever delirium found its way into his voice, the fighting spark in his brain remained sane. The igloo and the starving woman whom Blake had abandoned formed the one living picture which he did not for a moment forget. He must find the igloo, and the igloo was close to the sea. He could not miss it-- if he lived long enough to travel thirty miles. It did not occur to him that Blake might have lied-- that the igloo was farther than he had said, or perhaps much nearer.

It was two o'clock when he stopped to make tea. He figured that he had traveled at least eighteen miles; the fact was he had gone but a little over half that distance. He was not hungry, and ate nothing, but he fed Kazan heartily of meat. The hot tea, strengthened with a little whisky, revived him for the time more than food would have done.

"Twelve miles more at the most," he said to Kazan. "We'll make it. Thank God, we'll make it!"

If his eyes had been better he would have seen and recognized the huge snow-covered rock called the Blind Eskimo, which was just nine miles from the cabin. As it was, he went on, filled with hope. There were sharper pains in his head now, and his legs dragged wearily. Day ended at a little after two, but at this season there was not much change in light and darkness, and Pelliter scarcely noted the difference. The time came when the picture of the igloo and the dying woman came and went fitfully in his brain. There were dark spaces. The fighting spark was slowly giving way, and at last Pelliter dropped upon the sledge.

"Go on, Kazan!" he cried, weakly. "Mush it-- go on!"

Kazan tugged, with gaping jaws; and Pelliter's head dropped upon the food-filled pack.

What Kazan heard was a groan. He stopped and looked back, whining softly. For a time he sat on his haunches, sniffing a strange thing which had come to him in the air. Then he went on, straining a little faster at the sledge and still whining. If Pelliter had been conscious he would have urged him straight ahead. But old Kazan turned away from the sea. Twice in the next ten minutes he stopped and sniffed the air, and each time he changed his course a little. Half an hour later he came to a white mound that rose up out of the level waste of snow, and then he settled himself back on his haunches, lifted his shaggy head to the dark night sky, and for the second time that day he sent forth the weird, wailing, mourning death-howl.

It aroused Pelliter. He sat up, rubbed his eyes, staggered to his feet, and saw the mound a dozen paces away. Rest had cleared his brain again. He knew that it was an igloo. He could make out the door, and he caught up his lantern and stumbled toward it. He wasted half a dozen matches before he could make a light. Then he crawled in, with Kazan still in his traces close at his heels.

There was a musty, uncomfortable odor in the snow-house. And there was no sound, no movement. The lantern lighted up the small interior, and on the floor Pelliter made out a heap of blankets and a bearskin. There was no life, and instinctively he turned his eyes down to Kazan. The dog's head was stretched out toward the blankets, his ears were alert, his eyes burned fiercely, and a low, whining growl rumbled in his throat.

He looked at the blankets again, moved slowly toward them. He pulled back the bearskin and found what Blake had told him he would find-- a woman. For a moment he stared, and then a low cry broke from his lips as he fell upon his knees. Blake had not lied, for it was an Eskimo woman. She was dead. She had not died of starvation. Blake had killed her!

He rose to his feet again and looked about him. After all, did that golden hair, that white woman's hair, mean nothing? What was that? He sprang back toward Kazan, his weakened nerves shattered by a sound and a movement from the farthest and darkest part of the igloo. Kazan tugged at his traces, panting and whining, held back by the sledge wedged in the door. The sound came again, a human, wailing, sobbing cry.

With his lantern in his hand Pelliter darted across to it. There was another roll of blankets on the floor, and as he looked he saw the bundle move. It took him but an instant to drop beside it, as he had dropped beside the other, and as he drew back the damp and partly frozen covering his heart leaped up and choked him. The lantern light fell full upon the thin, pale face and golden head of a little child. A pair of big frightened eyes were staring up at him; and as he knelt there, powerless to move or speak in the face of this miracle, the eyes closed again, and there came again the wailing, hungry note which Kazan had first heard as they approached the igloo. Pelliter flung back the blanket and caught the child in his arms.

"It's a girl-- a little girl!" he almost shouted to Kazan. "Quick, boy-- go back-- get out!"

He laid the child upon the other blankets, and then thrust back Kazan. He seemed suddenly possessed of the strength of two men as he tore at his own blankets and dumped the contents of the pack out upon the snow. "She sent us, boy," he cried, his breath coming in sobbing gasps. "Where's the milk 'n' the stove--"

In ten seconds more he was back in the igloo with a can of condensed cream, a pan, and the alcohol lamp. His fingers trembled so that he had difficulty in lighting the wick, and as he cut open the can with his knife he saw the child's eyes flutter wide for an instant and then close again.

"Just a minute, a half minute," he pleaded, pouring the cream into the pan. "Hungry, eh, little one? Hungry? Starving ?" He held the pan close down over the blue liame and gazed terrified at the white little face near him. Its thinness and quiet frightened him. He thrust his finger into the cream and found it warm.

"A cup, Kazan! Why didn't I bring a cup?" He darted out again and returned with a tin basin. In another moment the child was in his arms, and he forced the first few drops of cream between her lips. Her eyes shot open. Life seemed to spring into her little body; and she drank with a loud noise, one of her tiny hands gripping him by the wrist. The touch, the sound, the feel of life against him thrilled Pelliter. He gave her half of what the basin contained, and then wrapped her up warmly in his thick service blanket, so that all of her was hidden but her face and her tangled golden hair. He held her for a moment close to the lantern. She was looking at him now, wide-eyed and wondering, but not frightened.

"God bless your little soul!" he exclaimed, his amazement growing. "Who are you, 'n' where'd you come from? You ain't more'n three years old, if you're an hour. Where's your mama 'n' your papa?" He placed her back on the blankets. "Now, a fire, Kazan!" he said.

He held the lantern above his head and found the narrow vent through the snow-and-ice wall which Blake had made for the escape of smoke. Then he went outside for the fuel, freeing Kazan on the way. In a few minutes more a small bright blaze of almost smokeless larchwood was lighting up and warming the interior of the igloo. To his surprise, Pelliter found the child asleep when he went to her again. He moved her gently and carried the dead body of the little Eskimo woman through the opening and half a hundred paces from the igloo. Not until then did he stop to marvel at the strength which had returned to him. He stretched his arms above his head and breathed deeply of the cold air. It seemed as though something had loosened inside of him, that a crushing weight had lifted itself from his eyes. Kazan had followed him, and he stared down at the dog.

"It's gone, Kazan," he cried, in a low, half-credulous voice. "I don't feel-- sick-- any more. It's her--"

He turned back to the igloo. The lantern and the fire made a cheerful glow inside, and it was growing warm. He threw off his heavy coat, drew the bearskin in front of the fire, and sat down with the child in his arms. She still slept. Like a starving man Pelliter stared down upon the little thin face. Gently his rough fingers stroked back the golden curls. He smiled. A light came into his eyes. His head bent lower and lower, slowly and a little fearfully. At last his lips touched the child's cheek. And then his own rough grizzled face, toughened by wind and storm and intense cold, nestled against the little face of this new and mysterious life he had found at the top of the world.

Kazan listened for a time, squatted on his haunches. Then he curled himself near the fire and slept. For a long time Pelliter sat rocking gently back and forth, thrilled by a happiness that was growing deeper and stronger in him each instant. He could feel the tiny beat of the little one's heart against his breast; he could feel her breath against his cheek; one of her little hands had gripped him by his thumb.

A hundred questions ran through his mind now. Who was this little abandoned mite? Who were her father and her mother, and where were they? How had she come to be with the Eskimo woman and Blake? Blake was not her father; the Eskimo woman was not her mother. What tragedy had placed her here? Somehow he was conscious of a sensation of joy as he reasoned that he would never be able to answer these questions. She belonged to him. He had found her. No one would ever come to dispossess him. Without awakening her, he thrust a hand into his breast pocket and drew out the photograph of the sweet-faced girl who was going to be his wife. It did not occur to him now that he might die. The old fear and the old sickness were gone. He knew that he was going to live.

"You," he breathed, softly, "you did it, and I know you'll be glad when I bring her down to you." And then to the little sleeping girl: "And if you ain't got a name I guess I'll have to call you Mystery-- how is that?-- my Little Mystery."

When he looked from the picture again Little Mystery's eyes were open and gazing up at him. He dropped the picture and made a lunge for the pan of cream warming before the fire. The child drank as hungrily as before, with Pelliter babbling incoherent nonsense into her baby ears. When she had done he picked up the photograph, with a sudden and foolish inspiration that she might understand.

"Looky," he cried. "Pretty--"

To his astonishment and joy, Little Mystery put out a hand and placed the tip of her tiny forefinger on the girl's face. Then she looked up into Pelliter's eyes.

"Mama," she lisped.

Pelliter tried to speak, but something rose like a knot in his throat and choked him. A fire leaped all at once through his body; the joy of that one word blinded him with hot tears. When he spoke at last his voice was broken, like a sobbing woman's.

"That's it." he said. "You're right, little one. She's your mama!"

IX
THE SECRET OF THE DEAD

On the eighth day after Pelliter found the Eskimo igloo Billy MacVeigh came up through a gray dawn with his footsore dogs, his letters, and his medicines. He had traveled all of the preceding night, and his feet dragged heavily. It was with a feeling of fear that he at last saw the black cliffs of Fullerton rising above the ice. He dreaded the first opening of the cabin door. What would he find? During the past forty-eight hours he had figured on Pelliter's chances, and they were two to one that he would find his partner dead in his bunk.

And if not, if Pelliter still lived, what a tale there would be to tell the sick man! For he knew that he must tell some one, and Pelliter would keep his secret. And he would understand. Day after day, as he had hurried straight into the north, Billy's loneliness and heartbreak weighed more and more heavily upon him. He tried to force Isobel out of his thoughts, but it was impossible. A thousand visions of her rose before him, and each mile that he drew himself farther away from her seemed only to add to the nearness of her spirit at his side and to the strange pain in his heart that rose now and then to his lips in sobbing breaths that he fought with himself to stifle. And yet, with his own grief and hopelessness, he experienced more and more each day a compensating joy. It was the joy of knowing that he had given back life and hope to Isobel and her husband. Each day he figured their progress along with his own. From the Eskimo village he had sent a messenger back to Churchill with a long report for the officer in command there, and in that report he had lied. He reported Scottie Deane as having died of the injury he had received in the snow-slide. Not for a moment had he regretted the falsehood. He also promised to report at Churchill to testify against Bucky Smith as soon as he reached Pelliter and put him on his feet.

On this last day, as he saw the towering cliffs of Fullerton ahead of him, he wondered how much he would tell to Pelliter if he found him alive. Mentally he rehearsed the amazing story of what came to him that night on the Barren, of the dogs coming across the snow, the great, dark, frightened eyes of the woman, and the long, narrow box on the sledge. He would tell pelliter all that. He would tell how he had made a camp for her that night, and how, later, he had told her that he loved her and had begged one kiss. And then the disclosures of the morning, the deserted tent, the empty box, the little note from Isobel, and the revelation that the box had contained the living body of the man for whom he and Pelliter had patrolled this desolate country for two thousand miles. But would he tell the truth of what had happened after that ?

He quickened his tired pace as the dogs climbed up from the ice of the Bay to the sloping ridge, and stared hard ahead of him. The dogs tugged harder as the smell of home entered their nostrils. At last the roof of the cabin came in view. MacVeigh's bloodshot eyes were like an animal's in their eagerness.

"Pelly, old boy," he gasped to himself. "Pelly--"

He stared harder. And then he spoke a low word to the dogs and stopped. He wiped his face. A deep breath of relief fell from his lips.

Straight up from the chimney of the cabin there rose a thick column of smoke!

He came up to the door of the cabin quietly, wondering why Pelliter did not see him or hear the three or four sharp yelps the dogs had given. He twisted off his snow-shoes, chuckling as he thought of the surprise he would give his mate. His hand was on the door latch when he stopped. The smile left his lips. Startled wonderment filled his face as he bent close to the door and listened, and for a moment his heart throbbed with a terrible fear. He had returned too late-- perhaps a day-- two days. Pelliter had gone mad! He could hear him raving inside, filling the cabin with a laughter that sent a chill of horror through his veins. Mad! A sob broke from his lips, and he turned his face up to the gray sky. And then the laughter turned to song. It was the sweet love song which Pelliter had told him that the girl down south used to sing to him when they were alone out under the stars. Suddenly it broke off short, and in its place he heard another sound. With a cry he opened the door and burst in.

"My God!" he cried. "Pelly-- Pelly--"

Pelliter was on his knees in the middle of the floor. But it was not the look of wonderment and joy in his face that Billy saw first. He stared at the little golden-haired creature on the floor in front of him. He had traveled hard, almost day and night, and for an instant it flashed upon him that what he saw was not real. Before he could move or speak again Pelliter was on his feet, wringing his hands and almost crying in his gladness. There was no sign of fever or madness in his face now. Like one in a dream Billy heard what he said.

"God bless you, Billy! I'm glad you've come!" he cried. "We've been waiting 'n' watching, and not more'n a minute ago we were at the window looking along the edge of the Bay through the binoculars. You must have been under the ridge. My God! A little while ago I thought I was dying-- I thought I was alone in the world-- alone-- alone. But look-- look, Billy, I've got a fam'ly!"

Little Mystery had climbed to her feet. She was looking at Billy wonderingly, her golden curls tousled about her pretty face, and gripping two or three of Pelliter's old letters in her tiny hand. And then she smiled at Billy and held out the letters to him. In an instant he had dropped Pelliter's hands and caught her up in his arms.

"I've got letters for you in my pocket, Pelly," he gasped. "But-- first-- you've got to tell me who she is and where you got her--"

Briefly Pelliter told of Blake's visit, the fight, and of the finding of Little Mystery.

"I'd have died if it hadn't been for her, Billy," he finished. "She brought me back to life. But I don't know who she is or where she came from. There wasn't anything in his pockets or in the igloo to tell. I buried him out there-- shallow-- so you could take a look when you came back."

He snatched like a starving man for food at the letters MacVeigh pulled from his pocket. While he read Billy sat down with Little Mystery on his knees. She laughed and put her warm little hands up to his rough face. Her eyes were blue, like Isobel's; and suddenly he crushed his face close down against her soft curls and held her so close to him that for a moment she was frightened. A little later Pelliter looked up. His eyes shone, his thin face was radiant with joy.

"God bless the sweetest little girl in the world, Billy!" he whispered, huskily.

"She says she's lonely for me. She tells me to hurry-- hurry down there to her. She says that if I don't come soon she'll come up to me! Read 'em, Billy!"

He looked in astonishment at the change which he saw in MacVeigh's face. Billy accepted the letters mechanically and placed them on the edge of the bunk near which he was sitting.

"I'll read them-- after a while," he said, slowly.

Little Mystery clambered from his knee and ran to Pelliter. Billy was staring straight into the other's face.

"You're sure you've told me everything, Pelly? There wasn't anything in his pockets? You searched well?"

"Yes. There was nothing."

"But-- you were sick--"

"That's why I buried him shallow," interrupted Pelliter. "He's close to the last cross, just under the ice and snow. I wanted you to look-- for yourself."

Billy rose to his feet. He took Little Mystery in his arms again and looked closely in her face. There was a strange look in his eyes. She laughed at him, but he did not seem to notice it. And then he held her out to Pelliter.

"Pelly, did you ever-- ever notice eyes-- very closely?" he asked. "Blue eyes?"

Pelliter stared at him amazed.

"My Jeanne has blue eyes--"

"And have they little brown dots in them like a wood violet?"

"No-o-o--"

"They're blue, just blue, ain't they?"

"Yes."

"And I suppose most all blue eyes are just blue, without the little brown spots. Wouldn't you think so?"

"What in Heaven's name are you driving at?" demanded Pelliter.

"I just wanted you to notice that her eyes have little brown spots in them," replied Billy. "I've only seen one other pair of eyes-- just like hers." He turned toward the door. "I'm going out to care for the dogs and dig up Blake," he added. "I can't rest until I've seen him."

Pelliter placed Little Mystery on her feet.

"I'll see to the dogs," he said. "But I don't want to look at Blake again."

The two men went out, and while Pelliter led the dogs to a lean-to behind the cabin Billy began to work with an ax and spade at the spot his comrade had pointed out to him. Ten minutes later he came to Blake. An excitement which he had tried to hide from Pelliter overcame his sense of horror as he dragged out the stiff and frozen corpse of the man. It was a terrible picture that the dead man made, with his coarse bearded face turned up to the sky and his teeth still snarling as they had snarled on the day he died. Billy knew most men who had come into the north above Churchill, but he had never looked upon Blake before. It was probable that the dead man had told a part of the truth, and that he was a sailor left on the upper coast by some whaler. He shivered as he began going through his pockets. Each moment added to his disappointment. He found a few things-- a knife, two keys, several coins, a fire-flint, and other articles-- but there was no letter or writing of any kind, and that was what he had hoped to find. There was nothing that might solve the mystery of the miracle that had descended upon them. He rolled the dead man into the grave, covered him over, and went into the cabin.

Pelliter was in his usual place-- on his hands and knees, with Little Mystery astride his back. He paused in a mad race across the cabin floor and looked up with inquiring eyes. The little girl held up her arms, and MacVeigh tossed her half-way to the ceiling and then hugged her golden head close up to his chilled face. Pelliter jumped to his feet; his face grew serious as Billy looked at him over the child's tousled curls.

"I found nothing-- absolutely nothing of any account," he said.

He placed Little Mystery on one of the bunks and faced the other with a puzzled loko in his eyes.

"I wish you hadn't been in a fever on that day of the fight, Pelly," he said. "He must have said something-- something that would give us a clue."

"Mebbe he did, Billy," replied Pelliter, looking with a shiver at the few things MacVeigh had placed on the cabin table. "But there's no use worrying any more about it. It ain't in reason that she's got any people up here, six hundred miles from the shack of a white man that 'd own a little beauty like her. She's mine. I found her. She's mine to keep."

He sat down at the table, and MacVeigh sat down opposite him, smiling sympathetically into Pelliter's eyes.

"I know you want her-- want her bad, Pelly," he said. "And I know the girl would love her. But she's got people-- somewhere, and it's our duty to find 'em. She didn't drop out of a balloon, Pelly. Do you suppose-- the dead man-- might be her father?"

It was the first time he had asked this question, and he noted the other's sudden shudder of revulsion.

"I've thought of that. But it can't be. He was a beast, and she-- she's a little angel. Billy, her mother must have been beautiful. had that's what made me guess-- fear--"

Pelliter wiped his face uneasily, and the two young men stared into each other's eyes. MacVeigh leaned forward, waiting.

"I figured it all out last night, lying awake there in my bunk," continued Pelliter, "and as the second best friend I have on earth I want to ask you not to go any farther, Billy. She's mine. My Jeanne, down there, will love her like a real mother, and we'll bring her up right. But if you go on, Billy, you'll find something unpleasant-- I-- I-- swear you will!"

"You know--"

"I've guessed," interrupted the other. "Billy, sometimes a beast-- a man beast-- holds an attraction for a woman, and Blake was that sort of a beast. You remember-- two years ago-- a sailor ran away with the wife of a whaler's captain away up at Narwhale Inlet. Well--"

Again the two men stared silently at each other. MacVeigh turned slowly toward the child. She had fallen asleep, and he could see the dull shimmer of her golden curls as they lay scattered over Pelliter's pillow.

"Poor little devil!" he exclaimed, softly.

"I believe that woman was Little Mystery's mother," Pelliter went on. "She couldn't bear to leave the little kid when she went with Blake, so she took her along. Some women do that. And after a time she died. Then Blake took up with an Eskimo woman. You know what happened after that. We don't want Little Mystery to know all this when she grows up. It's better not. She's too little to remember, ain't she? She won't ever know."

"I remember the ship," said Billy, not taking his eyes off Little Mystery. "She was the Silver Seal. Her captain's name was Thompson."

He did not look at Pelliter, but he could feel the quick, tense stiffening of the other's body. There was a moment's silence. Then Pelliter spoke in a low, unnatural voice.

"Billy, you ain't going to hunt him up, are you? That wouldn't be fair to me or to the kid. My Jeanne 'll love her, an' mebbe-- mebbe some day your kid 'll come along an' marry her--"

MacVeigh rose to his feet. Pelliter did not see the sudden look of grief that shot into his face.

"What do you say, Billy?"

"Think it over, Pelly," came back Billy's voice, huskily. "Think it over. I don't want to hurt you, and I know you think a lot of her, but-- think it over. You wouldn't rob her father, would you? An' she's all he's got left of the woman. Think it over, Pelly, good 'n' hard. I'm going to bed an' sleep a week!"

X
IN DEFIANCE OF THE LAW

Billy slept all that day and the night that followed, and Pelliter did not awaken him. He aroused himself from his long sleep of exhaustion an hour or two before dawn of the following morning, and for the first time he had the opportunity of going over with himself all the things that had happened since his return to Fullerton Point. His first thought was Pelliter and Little Mystery. He could hear his comrade's deep breathing in the bunk opposite him, and again he wondered if Pelliter had told him everything. Was it possible that Blake had said nothing to reveal Little Mystery's identity, and that the igloo and the dead Eskimo woman had not given up the secret ? It seemed inconceivable that there would not be something in the igloo that would help to clear up the mystery. And yet, after all, he had faith in Pelliter. He knew that he would keep nothing from him even though it meant possession of the child. And then his mind leaped to Isobel Deane. Her eyes were blue, and they had in them those same little spots of brown he had found in Little Mystery's. They were unusual eyes, and he had noticed the brown in them because it had added to their loveliness and had made him think of the violets he had told Pelliter about. Was it possible, he asked himself, that there could be some association between Isobel and Little Mystery ? He confessed that it was scarcely conceivable, and yet it was impossible for him to get the thought out of his mind.

Before Pelliter awoke he had determined upon his own course of action. He would say nothing of what had happened to himself on the Barren, at least not for a time. He would not tell of his meeting with Isobel and her husband or of what had followed. Until he was absolutely certain that Pelliter was keeping nothing from him he would not confide the secret of his own treachery to him. For he had been a traitor-- to the Law. He realized that. He could tell the story, with its fictitious ending, before they set out for Churchill, where he would give evidence against Bucky Smith. Meanwhile he would watch Pelliter, and wait for him to reveal whatever he might have hidden from him. He knew that if Pelliter was concealing something he was inspired by his almost insane worship of the little girl he had found who had saved him from madness and death. He smiled in the darkness as he thought that if Pelliter were working to achieve his own end-- possession of Little Mystery-- he was inspired by emotions no more selfish than his own in giving back life to Isobel Deane and her husband. On that score they were even.

He was up and had breakfast started before Pelliter awoke. Little Mystery was still sleeping, and the two men moved about softly in their moccasined feet. On this morning the sun shone brilliantly over the southern ice-fields, and Pelliter aroused Little Mystery so that she might see it before it disappeared. But to-day it did not drop below the gray murkiness of the snow-horizon for nearly an hour. After breakfast Pelliter read his letters again, and then Billy read them. In one of the letters the girl had put a tress of sunny hair, and Pelliter kissed it shamelessly before his comrade.

"She says she's making the dress she's going to wear when we're married, and that if I don't come home before it's out of style she'll never marry me at all," he cried, joyously. "Look there, on that page she's told me all about it. You're-- you're goin' to be there, ain't you, Billy?"

"If I can make it, Pelly."

"If you can make it! I thought you was going out of the Service when I did."

"I've sort of changed my mind."

"And you're going to stick ?"

"Mebbe for another three years."

Life in the cabin was different after this. Pelliter and Little Mystery were happy, and Billy fought with himself every hour to keep down his own gloom and despair. The sun helped him. It rose earlier each day and remained longer in the sky, and soon the warmth of it began to soften the snow underfoot. The vast fields of ice began to give evidence of the approach of spring, and the air was more and more filled with the thunderous echoes of the "break up." Great floes broke from the shore-runs, and the sea began to open. Down from the north the powerful arctic currents began to move their grinding, roaring avalanches. But it was a full month before Billy was sure that Pelliter was strong enough to begin the long trip south. Even then he waited for another week.

Late one afternoon he went out alone and stood on the cliff watching the thunderous movement of arctic ice out in the Roes Welcome. Standing motionless fifty paces from the little storm-beaten cabin that represented Law at this loneliest outpost on the American continent, he looked like a carven thing of dun-gray rock, with a dun-gray world over his head and on all sides of him, broken only in its terrific monotony of deathlike sameness by the darker gloom of the sky and the whiter and ghostlier gloom that hung over the ice-fields. The wind was still bitter, and his vision was shut in by a near horizon which Billy had often thought of as the rim of hell. On this afternoon his heart was as leaden as the day. Under his feet the frozen earth shivered with the rumbling reverberations of the crashing and breaking mountains of ice. His ears were filled with a dull and steady roar, like the echoes of distant thunder, broken now and then-- when an ice-mountain split asunder-- with a report like that of a thirteen-inch gun. There were curious wailings, strange screeching sounds, and heartbreaking moanings in the air. Two days before MacVeigh had heard the roar of the ice ten miles inland, where he had gone for caribou.

But he scarcely heard that roar now. He was looking toward the warring fields of ice, but he did not see them. It was not the dead gloom and the gray monotony that weighted his heart, but the sounds that he heard now and then in the cabin-- the laughing of Little Mystery and of Pelliter. A few days more and he would lose them. And after that what would be left for him? A cry broke from his lips, and he gripped his hands in despair. He would be alone. There was no one waiting for him down in that world to which Pelliter was going, no girl to meet him, no father, no mother-- nothing. He laughed in his pain as he faced the cold wind from the north. The sting of that wind was like the mocking ghost of his own past life. For all his life he had known only the stings of pain and of loneliness. And then, suddenly, there came Pelliter's words to him again-- "Mebbe some day you'll have a kid." A flood of warmth swept through his veins, and in the moment of forgetfulness and hope which came with it he turned his eyes into the south and west and saw the sweet face and upturned lips of Isobel Deane.

He pulled himself together with a low laugh and faced the breaking seas of ice and the north. The gloom of night had drawn the horizon nearer. The rumble and thunder of crumbling floes came from out of a purple chaos that was growing blue-black in the distance. For several minutes he stood listening and looking into nothingness. The breaking of the ice, the moaning discontent in the air, and the growling monotone of the giant currents had driven other men mad; but they held a fascination for him. He knew what was happening, and he could almost measure the strength of the unseen hands of nature. No sound was new or strange to him. But now, as he stood there, there rose above all the other tumult a sound that he had not heard before. His body became suddenly tense and alert as he faced squarely to the north. For a full minute he listened, and then turned and ran to the cabin.

Pelliter had lighted a lamp, and in its glow Billy's face shone white with excitement.

"Good God, Pelly, come here!" he cried from the door.

As Pelliter ran out he gripped him by the shoulders.

"Listen!" he commanded. "Listen to that!"

"Wolves!" said Pelliter.

The wind was rising, and sent a whistling blast through the open door of the cabin. It awakened Little Mystery, who sat up with frightened cries.

"No, it's not wolves," cried MacVeigh, and it did not sound like MacVeigh's voice that spoke. "I never heard wolves like that. Listen!"

He clutched Pelliter's arm as on a fresh burst of the wind there came the strange and terrible sound from out of the night. It was rapidly drawing nearer-- a wailing burst of savage voice, as if a great wolf pack had struck the fresh and blood-stained trail of game. But with this there was the other and more fearful sound, a shrieking and yelping as if half-human creatures were being torn by the fangs of beasts. As Pelliter and MacVeigh stood waiting for something to appear out of the gray-and-black mystery of the night they heard a sound that was like the slow tolling of a thing that was half bell and half drum.

"It's not wolves," shouted Billy. "Whatever it is, there's men with it! Hurry, Pelly, into the cabin with our dogs and sledge! Those are dogs we hear-- dogs who are howling because they smell us-- and there are hundreds of 'em! Where there's dogs there's men-- but who in Heaven's name can they be?"

He dragged the sledge into the cabin while Pelliter unleashed the huskies from the lean-to. When he came in with the dogs Pelliter locked and bolted the door.

Billy slipped a clipful of cartridges into his big-game Remington. His carbine was already on the table, and as Pelliter stood staring at him in indecision he pulled out two Savage automatics from under his bunk and gave one of them to his companion. His face was white and set.

"Better get ready, Pelly," he said, quietly. "I've been in this country a long time, and I tell you they're dogs and men. Did you hear the drum? It's made of seal belly, and there's a bell on each side of it. They're Eskimos, and there isn't an Eskimo village within two hundred miles of us this winter. They're Eskimos, and they're not on a hunt, unless it's for us!"

In an instant Pelliter was buckling on his revolver and cartridge-belt. He grinned as he looked at the wicked little blue-steeled Savage.

"I hope you ain't mistaken, Billy," he said, "for it 'll be the first excitement we've had in a year."

None of his enthusiasm revealed itself in MacVeigh's face.

"The Eskimo never fights until he's gone mad, Pelly," he said, "and you know what madmen are. I can't guess what they've got to fight over, unless they want our grub. But if they do--" He moved toward the door, his swift-firing Remington in his hand. "Be ready to cover me, Pelly. I'm going out. Don't fire until you hear me shoot."

He opened the door and stepped out. The howling had ceased now, but there came in its place strange barking voices and a cracking which Billy knew was made by the long Eskimo whips. He advanced to meet many dim forms which he saw breaking out of the wall of gloom, raising his voice in a loud holloa. From the Doorway Pelliter saw him suddenly lost in a mass of dogs and men, and half flung his carbine to his shoulder. But there was no shooting from MacVeigh. A score of sledges had drawn up about him, and the whips of dozens of little black men cracked viciously as their dogs sank upon their bellies in the snow. Both men and dogs were tired, and Billy saw that they had been running long and hard. Still as quick as animals the little men gathered about him, their white-and-black eyes staring at him out of round, thick, dumb-looking faces. He noted that they were half a hundred strong, and that all were armed, many with their little javelin-like narwhal harpoons, some with spears, and others with rifles. From the circle of strangely dressed and hideously visaged beings that had gathered about him one advanced and began talking to him in a language that was like the rapid clack of knuckle bones.

"Kogmollocks!" Billy groaned, and he lifted both hands to show that he did not understand. Then he raised his voice. "Nuna-talmute," he cried. "Nuna-talmute-- Nuna-talmute! Ain't there one of that lingo among you?"

He spoke directly to the chief man, who stared at him in silence for a moment and then pointed both short arms toward the lighted cabin.

"Come on!" said Billy. He caught the little Eskimo by one of his thick arms and led him boldly through the breach that was made for them in the circle. The chief man's voice broke out in a few words of command, like a dozen quick, sharp yelps of a dog, and six other Eskimos dropped in behind them.

"Kogmollocks-- the blackest-hearted little devils alive when it comes to trading wives and fighting," said MacVeigh to Pelliter, as he came up at the head of the seven little black men. " Watch the door, Pelly. They're coming in."

He stepped into the cabin, and the Eskimos followed. From Pelliter's bunk Little Mystery looked at the strange visitors with eyes which suddenly widened with surprise and joy, and in another moment she had given the strange story that Pelliter or Billy had ever heard her utter. Scarcely had that cry fallen from her lips when one of the Eskimos sprang toward her. His black hands were already upon her, dragging the child from the bunk, when with a warning yell of rage Pelliter leaped from the door and sent him crashing back among his companions. In another instant both men were facing the seven Eskimos with leveled automatics.

"If you fire don't shoot to kill!" commanded MacVeigh.

The chief man was pointing to Little Mystery, his weird voice rising until it was almost a scream. Suddenly he doubled himself back and raised his javelin. Simultaneously two streams of fire leaped from the automatics. The javelin dropped to the floor, and with a shrill cry which was half pain and half command the leader staggered back to the door, a stream of blood running from his wounded hand. The others sprang out ahead of him, and Pelliter closed and bolted the door. When he turned MacVeigh was closing and slipping the bolts to the heavy barricades of the two windows. From Pelliter's bunk Little Mystery looked at them and laughed.

"So it's you?" said Billy, coming to her, and breathing hard. "It's you they want, eh? Now, I wonder why ?"

Pelliter's face was flushed with excitement. He was reloading his automatic. There was almost a triumph in his eyes as he met MacVeigh's questioning gaze.

They stood and listened, heard only the rumbling monotone of the drifting ice-- not the breath of a sound from the scores of men and dogs.

"We've given them a lesson," said Pelliter, at last, smiling with the confidence of a man who was half a tenderfoot among the little brown men.

Billy pointed to the door.

"That door is about the only place vulnerable to their bullets," he said, as though he had not heard Pelliter. "Keep out of its range. I don't believe what guns they've got are heavy enough to penetrate the logs. Your bunk is out of line and safe."

He went to Little Mystery, and his stern face relaxed into a smile as she put up her arms to greet him.

"So it's you, is it ?" he asked again, taking her warm little face and soft curls between his two hands. "They want you, an' they want you bad. Well, they can have grub, an' they can have me, but"-- he looked up to meet Pelliter's eyes-- "I'm damned if they can have you," he finished.

Suddenly the night was broken by another sound, the sharp, explosive crack of rifles. They could hear the beat of bullets against the log wall of the cabin. One crashed through the door, tearing away a splinter as wide as a man's arm, and as MacVeigh nodded to the path of the bullet he laughed. Pelliter had heard that laugh before. He knew what it meant. He knew what the death-whiteness of MacVeigh's face meant. It was not fear, but something more terrible than fear. His own face was flushed. That is the difference in men.

MacVeigh suddenly darted across the danger zone to the opposite half of the cabin.

"If that's your game, here goes," he cried. "Now, damn y', you're so anxious to fight-- get at it 'n' fight!"

He spoke the last words to Pelliter. Billy always swore when he went into action.

XI
THE NIGHT OF PERIL

On his own side of the cabin Pelliter began tugging at a small, thin block laid between two of the logs. The shooting outside had ceased when the two men opened up the loopholes that commanded a range seaward. Almost immediately it began again, the dull red flashes showing the location of the Eskimos, who had drawn back to the ridge that sloped down to the Bay. As the last of five shots left his Remington Billy pulled in his gun and faced across to Pelliter, who was already reloading.

"Pelly, I don't want to croak," he said, "but this is the last of Law at Fullerton Point-- for you and me. Look at that!"

He raised the muzzle of his rifle to one of the logs over his head. Pelliter could see the fresh splinters sticking out.

"They've got some heavy calibers," continued Billy, "and they've hidden behind the slope, where they're safe from us for a thousand years. As soon as it grows light enough to see they'll fill this shack as full of holes as an old cheese."

As if to verify his words a single shot rang out and a bullet plowed through a log so close to Pelliter that the splinters flew into his face.

"I know these little devils, Pelly," went on MacVeigh. "If they were Nunatalmutes you could scare 'em with a sky-rocket. But they're Kogmollocks. They've murdered the crews of half a dozen whalers, and I shouldn't wonder if they'd got the kid in some such way. They wouldn't let us off now, even if we gave her up. It wouldn't do. They know better than to let the Law get any evidence against them. If we're killed and the cabin burned, who's going to say what happened to us ? There's just two things for us to do--"

Another fusillade of shots came from the snow ridge, and a third bullet crashed into the cabin.

"Just two things," Billy went on, as he completely shaded the dimly burning lamp. "We can stay here 'n' die-- or run."

"Run!"

This was an unknown word in the Service, and in Pelliter's voice there were both amazement and contempt.

"Yes, run," said Billy, quietly. "Run-- for the kid's sake."

It was almost dark in the cabin, and Pelliter came close to his companion.

"You mean--"

"That it's the only way to save the kid. We might give her up, then fight it out, but that means she'd go back to the Eskimos, 'n' mebbe never be found again. The men and dogs out there are bushed. We are fresh. If we can get away from the cabin we can beat 'em out."

"We'll run, then," said Pelliter. He went to Little Mystery, who sat stunned into silence by the strange things that were happening, and hugged her up in his arms, his back turned to the possible bullet that might come through the wall. "We're going to run, little sweetheart," he mumbled, half laughingly, in her curls.

Billy began to pack, and Pelliter put Little Mystery down on the bunk and started to harness the six dogs, ranging them close along the wall, with old one-eyed Kazan, the hero who had saved him from Blake, in the lead. Outside the firing had ceased. It was evident that the Eskimos had made up their minds to save their ammunition until dawn.

Fifteen minutes sufficed to load the sledge; and while Pelliter was fastening the sledge traces MacVeigh bundled Little Mystery into her thick fur coat. The sleeves caught, and he turned it back, exposing the white edge of the lining. On that lining was something which drew him down close, and when the strange cry that fell from his lips drew Pelliter's eyes toward him he was staring down into Little Mystery's upturned face with the look of one who saw a vision.

"Mother of Heaven!" he gasped, "she's--" He caught himself, and smothered Little Mystery up close to him for a moment before he brought her to the sledge. "She's the bravest little kid in the world," he finished; and Pelliter wondered at the strangeness of his voice. He tucked her into a nest made of blankets and then tied her in securely with babiche rope. Pelliter stood up first and saw the hungry, staring look in MacVeigh's face as he kept his eyes steadily upon Little Mystery.

"What's the matter, Mac?" he asked. "Are you very much afraid-- for her ?"

"No," said MacVeigh, without lifting his head. "If you're ready, Pelly, open the door." He rose to his feet and picked up his rifle. He did not seem like the old MacVeigh; but the dogs were nipping and whining, and there was no time for Pelliter's questions.

"I'm going out first, Billy," he said. "You can make up your mind they're watching the cabin pretty close, and as soon as the dogs nose the open air they'll begin yapping 'n' let 'em on to us. We can't risk her under fire. So I'm going to back along the edge of the ridge and give it to 'em as fast as I can work the gun. They'll all turn to me, and that's the time for you to open the door and make your getaway. I'll be with you inside of five minutes."

He turned out the lights as he spoke. Then he opened the door and slipped out into the darkness without a protesting word from MacVeigh. Hardly had he gone when the latter fell upon his knees beside Little Mystery and in the deep gloom crushed his rough face down against her soft, warm little body.

"So it's you, is it?" he cried, softly; and then he mumbled things which the little girl could not possibly have understood.

Suddenly he sprang to his feet and ran to the door with a word to faithful old Kazan, the leader.

From far down the snow-ridge there came the rapid firing of Pelliter's rifle.

For a moment Billy waited, his hand on the door, to give the watching Eskimos time to turn their attention toward Pelliter. He could perhaps have counted fifty before he gave Kazan the leash and the six dogs dragged the sledge out into the night. With his humanlike intelligence old Kazan swung quickly after his master, and the team darted like a streak into the south and west, giving tongue to that first sharp, yapping voice which it is impossible to beat or train out of a band of huskies. As he ran Billy looked back over his shoulder. In the hundred-yard stretch of gray bloom between the cabin and the snow-ridge he saw three figures speeding like wolves. In a flash the meaning of this unexpected move of the Eskimos dawned upon him. They were cutting Pelliter off from the cabin and his course of flight.

"Go it, Kazan!" he cried, fiercely, bending low over the leader. "Moo-hoosh-- moo-hoosh-- moo-hoosh, old man!" And Kazan leaped into a swift run, nipping and whining at the empty air.

Billy stopped and whirled about. Two other figures had joined the first three, and he opened fire. One of the running Eskimos pitched forward with a cry that rose shrill and scarcely human above the moaning and roar of the ice-fields, and the other four fell flat upon the snow to escape the hail of lead that sang close over their heads. From the snow-ridge there came a fusillade of shots, and a single figure darted like a streak in MacVeigh's direction. He knew that it was Pelliter; and, running slowly after Kazan and the sledge, he rammed a fresh clipful of cartridges into the chamber of his rifle. The figures in the open had risen again, and Pelliter's automatic Savage trailed out a stream of fire as he ran. He was breathing heavily when he reached Billy.

"Kazan has got the kid well in the lead," shouted the latter. "God bless that old scoundrel! I believe he's human."

They set off swiftly, and the thick night soon engulfed all signs of the Eskimos. Ahead of them the sledge loomed up slowly, and when they reached it both men thrust their rifles under the blanket straps. Thus relieved of their weight, they forged ahead of Kazan.

"Moo-hoosh-- moo-hoosh!" encouraged Billy.

He glanced at Pelliter on the opposite side. His comrade was running with one arm raised at the proper angle to reserve breath and endurance; the other hung straight and limp at his side. A sudden fear shot through him, and he darted ahead of the lead dog to Pelliter's side. He did not speak, but touched the other's arm.

"One of the little devil's winged me," gasped Pelliter. "It's not bad."

He was breathing as though the short run was already winding him, and without a word Billy ran up to Kazan's head and stopped the team within twenty paces. The open blade of his knife was ripping up Pelliter's sleeve before his comrade could find words to object. Pelliter was bleeding, and bleeding hard. His face was shot with pain. The bullet had passed through the fleshy part of his forearm, but had fortunately missed the main artery. With the quick deftness of the wilderness-trained surgeon Billy drew the wound close and bound it tightly with his own and Pelliter's handkerchiefs. Then he thrust Pelliter toward the sledge.

"You've got to ride, Pelly," he said. "If you don't you'll go under, and that means all of us."

Far behind them there rose the yapping and howling of dogs.

"They're after us with the dogs!" groaned Pelliter. "I can't ride. I've got to run--and fight!"

"You get on the sledge, or I'll stave your head in!" commanded MacVeigh. "Face the enemy, Pelly, and give 'em hell. You've got three rifles there. You can do the shooting while I hustle on the dogs. And keep yourself in front of her," he added, pointing to the almost completely buried Little Mystery.

XII
LITTLE MYSTERY FINDS HER OWN

After convincing Pelliter that he must ride on the sledge Billy ran on ahead, and the dogs started with their heavier load.

"Now for the timber-line," he called down to Kazan. "It's fifty miles, old boy, and you've got to make it by dawn. If we don't--"

He left the words unfinished, but Kazan tugged harder, as if he had heard and understood. The sledge had reached the unbroken sweep of the Barren now, and MacVeigh felt the wind in his face. It was blowing from the north and west, and with it came sudden gusts filled with fine particles of snow. After a few moments he fell back to see that Little Mystery's face was completely covered. Pelliter was crouching low on the sledge, his feet braced in the blanket straps. His wound and the uncomfortable sensation of riding backward on a swaying sledge were making him dizzy, and he wondered if what he saw creeping up out of the night was a result of this dizziness or a reality. There was no sound from behind. But a darker spot had grown within his vision, at times becoming larger, then almost disappearing. Twice he raised his rifle. Twice he lowered it again, convinced that the thing behind was only a shadowy fabric of his imagination. It was possible that their pursuers would lose trace of them in the darkness, and so he held his fire.

He was staring at the shadow when from out of it there leaped a little spurt of flame, and a bullet sang past the sledge, a yard to the right. It was a splendid shot. There was a marksman with the shadow, and Pelliter replied so quickly that the first shot had not died away before there followed the second. Five times his automatic sent its leaden messengers back into the night, and at the fifth shot there came a wild outburst of pain from one of the Eskimo dogs.

"Hurrah!" shouted Billy. "That's one team out of business, Pelly. We can beat 'em in a running fight!"

He heard the quick metallic snap of fresh cartridges as Pelliter slipped them into the chamber of his rifle, but beyond that sound, the wind, and the straining of the huskies there was no other. A grim silence fell behind. The roar of the distant ice grew less. The earth no longer seemed to shudder under their feet at the terrific explosions of the crumbling bergs. But in place of these the wind was rising and the fine snow was thickening. Billy no longer turned to look behind. He stared ahead and as far as he could see on each side of them. At the end of half an hour the panting dogs dropped into a walk, and he walked close beside his comrade.

"They've given it up," groaned Pelliter, weakly. "I'm glad of it, Mac, for I'm-- I'm-- dizzy." He was lying on the sledge now, with his head bolstered up on a pile of blankets.

"You know how the wolves hunt, Pelly," said MacVeigh-- "in a moon-shape half circle, you know, that closes in on the running game from in front? Well, that's how the Eskimos hunt, and I'm wondering if they're trying to get ahead of us-- off there, and off there." He motioned to the north and the south.

"They can't," replied Pelliter, raising himself to his elbow with an effort. "Their dogs are bushed. Let me walk, Mac. I can--" He fell back with a sudden low cry. "Gawd, but I'm dizzy--"

MacVeigh halted the dogs, and while they dropped upon their bellies, panting and licking up the snow, he kneeled beside Pelliter. Darkness concealed the fear in his eyes and face. His voice was strong and cheerful.

"You've got to lie still, Pelly," he warned, arranging the blankets so that the wounded man could rest comfortably. "You've got a pretty bad nip, and it's best for all of us that you don't make a move. You're right about the Eskimos and their dogs. They're bushed, and they've given the chase up as a bad job, so what's the use of making a fool of yourself? Ride it out, Pelly. Go to sleep with Little Mystery if you can. She thinks she's in a cradle."

He got up and started the dogs. For a long time he was alone. Little Mystery was sleeping and Pelliter was quiet. Now and then he dropped his mittened hand on Kazan's head, and the faithful old leader whined softly at his touch. With the others it was different. They snapped viciously, and he kept his distance. He went on for hours, halting the team now and then for a few minutes' rest. He struck a match each time and looked at Pelliter. His comrade breathed heavily, with his eyes closed. Once, long after midnight, he opened them and stared at the flare of the match and into MacVeigh's white face.

"I'm all right, Billy," he said. "Let me walk--"

MacVeigh forced him back gently, and went on. He was alone until the first cold, gray break of dawn. Then he stopped, gave each of the dogs a frozen fish, and with the fuel on the sledge built a small fire. He scraped up snow for tea, and hung the pail over the fire. He was frying bacon and toasting hard bannock biscuits when Pelliter aroused himself and sat up. Billy did not see him until he faced about.

"Good morning, Pelly," he grinned. "Have a good nap?"

Pelliter groped about on the sledge.

"Wish I could find a club," he growled. "I'd-- I'd brain you! You let me sleep!"

He thrust out his uninjured arm, and the two shook hands. Once or twice before they had done this after hours of great peril. It was not an ordinary handshake.

Billy rose to his feet. Half a mile away the edge of the big forest for which they had been fighting rose out of the dawn gloom.

"If I'd known that," he said, pointing, "we'd have camped in shelter. Fifty miles, Pelly. Not so bad, was it?"

Behind them the gray Barren was lifting itself into the light of day. The two men ate and drank tea. During those few minutes neither gave attention to the forest or the Barren. Billy was ravenously hungry. Pelliter could not get enough of the tea. And then their attention went to Little Mystery, who awoke with a wailing protest at the smothering cover of blankets over her face. Billy dug her out and held her up to view the strange change since yesterday. It was then that Kazan stopped licking his ashy chops to send up a wailing howl.

Both men turned their eyes toward the forest. Halfway between a figure was toiling slowly toward them. It was a man, and Billy gave a low cry of astonishment.

But Kazan was facing the gray Barren, and he howled again, long and menacingly. The other dogs took up the cry, and when Pelliter and MacVeigh followed the direction of their warning they stood for a full quarter of a minute as if turned into stone.

A mile away the Barren was dotted with a dozen swiftly moving sledges and a score of running men!

After all, their last stand was to be made at the edge of the timber-line!

In such situations men like MacVeigh and Pelliter do not waste precious moments in prearranging actions in words. Their mental processes are instantaneous and correlative-- and they act. Without a word Billy replaced Little Mystery in her nest without even giving her a sip of the warm tea, and by the time the dogs were straightened in their traces Pelliter was handing him his Remington.

"I've ranged it for three hundred and fifty yards," he said. "We won't want to waste our fire until they come that near."

They set out at a trot, Pelliter running with his wounded arm down at his side. Suddenly the lone figure between them and the forest disappeared. It had fallen flat in the snow, where it lay only a black speck. In a moment it rose again and advanced. Both Pelliter and Billy were looking when it fell for a second time.

An unpleasant laugh came from MacVeigh's lips.

The figure was climbing to its feet for the fifth time, and was only on its hands and knees when the sledge drew up. It was a white man. His head was bare, his face deathlike. His neck was open to the cold wind, and, to the others' astonishment, he wore no heavier garment over his dark flannel shirt. His eyes burned wildly from out of a shaggy growth of beard and hair, and he was panting like one who had traveled miles instead of a few hundred yards.

All this Billy saw at a glance, and then he gave a sudden unbelieving cry. The man's red eyes rested on his, and every fiber in his body seemed for a moment to have lost the power of action. He gasped and stared, and Pelliter started as if stung at the words which came first from his lips.

"Deane-- Scottie Deane!"

An amazed cry broke from Pelliter. He looked at MacVeigh, his chief. He made an involuntary movement forward, but Billy was ahead of him. He had flung down his rifle, and in an instant was on his knees at Deane's side, supporting his emaciated figure in his arms.

"Good God! what does this mean, old man?" he cried, forgetting Pelliter. "What has happened? Why are you away up here? And where-- where-- is she?"

He had gripped Deane's hand. He was holding him tight; and Deane, looking up into his eyes, saw that he was no longer looking into the face of the Law, but that of a brother. He smiled feebly.

"Cabin-- back there-- in edge-- woods," he gasped. "Saw you-- coming. Thought mebbe you'd pass-- so-- came out. I'm done for-- dying."

He drew a deep breath and tried to assist himself as Billy raised him to his feet. A little wailing cry came from the sledge. Startled, Deane turned his eyes toward that cry.

"My God!" he screamed.

He tore himself away from Billy and flung himself upon his knees beside Little Mystery, sobbing and talking like a madman as he clasped the frightened child in his arms. With her he leaped to his feet with new strength.

"She's mine-- mine!" he cried, fiercely. "She's what brought me back! I was going for her! Where did you get her? How--"

There came to them now in sudden chorus the wild voice of the Eskimo dogs out on the plain. Deane heard the cry and faced with the others in their direction. They were not more than half a mile away, bearing down upon them swiftly. Billy knew that there was not a moment to lose. In a flash it had leaped upon him that in some way Deane and Isobel and Little Mystery were associated with that avenging horde, and as quickly as he could he told Deane what had happened. Sanity had come back into Deane's eyes, and no sooner had he heard than he ran out in the face of the army of little brown men with Little Mystery in his arms. MacVeigh and Pelliter could hear him calling to them from a distance. They were in the edge of the forest when Deane met the Eskimos. There was a long wait, and then Deane and Little Mystery came back-- on a sledge drawn by Eskimo dogs. Beside the sledge walked the chief who had been wounded in the cabin at Fullerton Point. Deane was swaying, his head was bowed half upon his breast, and the chief and another Eskimo were supporting him. He nodded to the right, and a hundred yards away they found a cabin. The powerful little northerners carried him in, still clutching Little Mystery in his arms, and he made a motion for Billy to follow him-- alone. Inside the cabin they placed him on a low bunk, and with a weak cough he beckoned Billy to his side. MacVeigh knew what that cough meant. The sick man had suffered terrible exposure, and the tissue of his lungs was sloughing away. It was death, the most terrible death of the north.

For a few moments Deane lay panting, clasping one of Billy's hands. Little

Mystery slipped to the floor and began to investigate the cabin. Deane smiled into Billy's eyes.

"You've come again-- just in time," he said, quite steadily. "Seems queer, don't it, Billy?"

For the first time he spoke the other's name as if he had known him a lifetime. Billy covered him over gently with one of the blankets, and in spite of himself his eyes sought about him questioningly. Deane saw the look.

"She didn't come," he whispered. "I left her--"

He broke off with a racking cough that brought a crimson stain to his lips. Billy felt a choking grief.

"You must be quiet," he said. "Don't try to talk now. You have no fire, and I will build one. Then I'll make you something hot."

He went to move away, but one of Deane's hands detained him.

"Not until I've said something to you, Billy," he insisted. "You know-- you understand. I'm dying. It's liable to come any minute now, and I've got to tell you-- things. You must understand-- before I go. I won't be long. I killed a man, but I'm-- not sorry. He tried to insult her-- my wife-- an' you-- you'd have killed him, too. You people began to hunt me, and for safety we went far north-- among the Eskimos-- an' lived there-- long time. The Eskimos-- they loved the little girl an' wife, specially little Isobel. Thought them angels-- some sort. Then we heard you were goin' to hunt for me-- up there-- among the Eskimos. So we set out with the box. Box was for her-- to keep her from fearful cold. We didn't dare take the baby-- so we left her up there. We were going back-- soon-- after you'd made your hunt. When we saw your fire on the edge of the Barren she made me get in the box-- an' so-- so you found us. You know-- after that. You thought it was-- coffin-- an' she told you I was dead. You were good-- good to her-- an' you must go down there where she is, and take little Isobel. We were goin' to do as you said-- an' go to South America. But we had to have the baby, an' I came back. Should have told you. We knew that-- afterward. But we were afraid-- to tell the secret-- even to you--"

He stopped, panting and coughing. Billy was crushing both his thin, cold hands in his own. He found no word to say. He waited, fighting to stifle the sobbing grief in his breath.

"You were good-- good-- good-- to her," repeated Deane, weakly, "You loved her-- an' it was right-- because you thought I was dead an' she was alone an' needed help. I'm glad-- you love her. You've been good-- 'n' honest-- an I want some one like you to love her an' care for her. She ain't got nobody but me-- an' little Isobel. I'm glad-- glad-- I've found a man-- like you!"

He suddenly wrenched his hands free and took Billy's tense face between them, staring straight into his eyes.

"An'-- an'-- I give her to you," he said. "She's an angel, and she's alone-- needs some one-- an' you-- you'll be good to her. You must go down to her-- Pierre Couchée's cabin-- on the Little Beaver. An' you'll be good to her-- good to her--"

"I will go to her," said Billy, softly. "And I swear here on my knees before the great and good God that I will do what an honorable man should do!"

Deane's rigid body relaxed, and he sank back on his blankets with a sigh of relief.

"I worried-- for her," he said. "I've always believed in a God-- though I killed a man-- an' He sent you here in time!" A sudden questioning light came into his eyes. "The man who stole little Isobel," he breathed-- "who was he?"

"Pelliter-- the man out there-- killed him when he came to the cabin," said Billy. "He said his name was Blake-- Jim Blake."

"Blake! Blake! Blake!" Again Deane's voice rose from the edge of death to a shriek. "Blake, you say? A great coarse sailorman, with red hair-- red beard-- yellow teeth like a walrus! Blake-- Blake--" He sank back again, with a thrilling, half-mad laugh. "Then-- then it's all been a mistake-- a funny mistake," he said; and his eyes closed, and his voice spoke the words as though he were uttering them from out of a dream.

Billy saw that the end was near. He bent down to catch the dying man's last words. Deane's hands were as cold as ice. His lips were white. And then Deane whispered:

"We fought-- I thought I killed him-- an' threw him into the sea. His right name was Samuelson. You knew him-- by that name-- but he went often-- by Blake-- Jim Blake. So-- so-- I'm not a murderer-- after all. An' he-- he came back for revenge-- and-- stole-- little-- Isobel. I'm-- I'm-- not-- a-- murderer. You-- you-- will-- tell-- her. You'll tell her-- I didn't kill him-- after all. You'll tell her-- an'-- be-- good-- good--"

He smiled. Billy bent lower.

"Again I swear before the good God that I will do what an honorable man should do," he replied.

Deane made no answer. He did not hear. The smile did not fade entirely from his lips. But Billy knew that in this moment death had come in through the cabin door. With a groan of anguish he dropped Deane's stiffening hand. Little Isobel pattered across the floor to his side. She laughed; and suddenly Billy turned and caught her in his arms, and, crumpled down there on the floor beside the one brother he had known in life, he sobbed like a woman.

XIII
THE TWO GODS

It was little Isobel who pulled MacVeigh together, and after a little he rose with her in his arms and turned her from the wall while he covered Deane's face with the end of a blanket. Then he went to the door. The Eskimos were building fires. Pelliter was seated on the sledge a short distance from the cabin, and at Billy's call he came toward him.

"If you don't mind, you can take her over to one of the fires for a little while," said Billy. "Scottie is dead. Try and make the chief understand,"

He did not wait for Pelliter to question him, but closed the door quietly and went back to Deane. He drew off the blanket and gazed for a moment into the still, bearded face.

"My Gawd, an' she's waitin' for you, 'n' looking for you, an' thinks you're coming back soon," he whispered. "You 'n' the kid!"

Reverently he began the task ahead of him. One after another he went into Deane's pockets and drew forth what he found. In one pocket there was a small knife, some cartridges, and a match box. He knew that Isobel would prize these and keep them because her husband had carried them, and he placed them in a handkerchief along with other things he found. Last of all he found in Deane's breast pocket a worn and faded envelope. He peered into the open end before he placed it on the little pile, and his heart gave a sudden throb when he saw the blue flower petals Isobel had given him. When he was done he crossed Deane's hands upon his breast. He was tying the ends of the handkerchief when the door opened softly behind him.

The little dark chief entered. He was followed by four other Eskimos. They had left their weapons outside. They seemed scarcely to breathe as they ranged themselves in a line and looked down upon Scottie Deane. Not a sign of emotion came into their expressionless faces, not the flicker of an eyelash did the immobility of their faces change. In a low, clacking monotone they began to speak, and there was no expression of grief in their voices. Yet Billy understood now that in the hearts of these little brown men Scottie Deane stood enshrined like a god. Before he was cold in death they had come to chant his deeds and his virtues to the unseen spirits who would wait and watch at his side until the beginning of the new day. For ten minutes the monotone continued. Then the five men turned and without a word, without looking at him, went out of the cabin. Billy followed them, wondering if Deane had convinced them that he and Pelliter were his friends. If he had not done that he feared that there would still be trouble over little Isobel. He was delighted when he found Pelliter talking with one of the men.

"I've found a flunkey here whose lingo I can get along with," cried Pelliter. "I've been telling 'em what bully friends we are, and have made 'em understand all about Blake. I've shaken hands with them all three or four times, and we feel pretty good. Better mix a little. They don't like the idea of giving us the kid, now that Scottie's dead. They're asking for the woman."

Half an hour later MacVeigh and Pelliter returned to the cabin. At the end of that time he was confident that the Eskimos would give them no further trouble and that they expected to leave Isobel in their possession. The chief, however, had given Billy to understand that they reserved the right to bury Deane.

Billy felt that he was now in a position where he would have to tell Pelliter some of the things that had happened to him on his return to Churchill. He had reported Deane's death as having occurred weeks before as the result of a fall, and when he returned to Fort Churchill he knew that he would have to stick to that story. Unless Pelliter knew of Isobel, his love for her, and his own defiance of the Law in giving them their freedom, his comrade might let out the truth and ruin him.

In the cabin they sat down at the table. Pelliter's arm was in a sling. His face was drawn and haggard and blackened by powder. He drew his revolver, emptied it of cartridges, and gave it to little Isobel to play with. He kept up his spirits among the Eskimos, but he made no effort to conceal his dejection now.

"I've lost her," he said, looking at Billy. "You're going to take her to her mother?"

"Yes."

"It hurts. You don't know how it's goin' to hurt to lose her," he said.

MacVeigh leaned across the table and spoke earnestly.

"Yes, I know what it means, Pelly," he replied. "I know what it means to love some one-- and lose. I know. Listen."

Quickly he told Pelliter the story of the Barren, of the coming of Isobel, the mother, of the kiss she had given him, and of the flight, the pursuit, the recapture, and of that final moment when he had taken the steel cuffs from Deane's wrists. Once he had begun the story he left nothing untold, even to the division of the blue-flower petals and the tress of Isobel's hair. He drew both from his pocket and showed them to Pelliter, and at the tremble in his voice there came a mistiness in his comrade's eyes. When he had finished Pelliter reached across with his one good arm and gripped the other's hand.

"An' what she said about the blue flower is comin' true, Billy," he whispered. "It's bringing happiness to you, just as she said, for you're going down to her--"

MacVeigh interrupted him.

"No, it's not," he said, softly. "She loved him-- as much as the girl down there will ever love you, Pelly, and when I tell her what has happened-- her heart will break. That can't bring happiness-- for me !"

The hours of that day bore leaden weights for Billy. The two men made their plans. A number of the Eskimos agreed to accompany Pelliter as far as Eskimo Point, whence he would make his way alone to Churchill. Billy would strike south to the Little Beaver in search of Couchée's cabin and Isobel. He was glad when night came. It was late when he went to the door, opened it, and looked out.

In the edge of the timber-line it was black, black not only with the gloom of night, but with the concentrated darkness of spruce and balsam and a sky so low and thick that one could almost hear the wailing swish of it overhead like the steady sobbing of surf on a seashore. It was black, save for the small circles of light made by the Eskimo fires, about which half a hundred of the little brown men sat or crouched. The masters of the camp were all awake, but twice as many dogs, exhausted and footsore, lay curled in heaps, as inanimate as if dead. There was present a strange silence and a strange and unnatural gloom that was not of the night alone, a silence broken only by the low moaning of the wind out on the Barren, the restlessness in the air above the tree-tops, and the crackling of the fires. The Eskimos were as motionless as so many dead men. Their round, expressionless eyes were wide open. They sat or crouched with their backs to the Barren, their faces turned into the still deeper blackness of the forest. Some distance away, like a star, there gleamed the small and steady light in the cabin window. For two hours the eyes of those about the fires had been fixed on that light. And at intervals there had risen from among the stony-faced watchers the little chief, whose clacking voice joined for a few moments each time the wailing of the wind, the swish of the low-hanging sky, and the crackling of the fires. But there was sound of no other voice or movement. He alone moved and spoke, for to the others the clacking sounds he made was speech, words spoken each time for the man who lay dead in the cabin.

A dozen times Pelliter and MacVeigh had looked out to the fires, and looked each time at the hour. This time Billy said:

"They're moving, Pelly! They're jumping to their feet and coming this way!" He looked at his watch again. "They're mighty good guessers. It's a quarter after twelve. When a chief or a big man dies they bury him in the first hour of the new day. They're coming after Deane."

He opened the door and stepped out into the night. Pelliter joined him. The Eskimos advanced without a sound and stopped in a shadowy group twenty paces from the cabin. Five of these little fur-clad men detached themselves from the others and filed into the cabin, with the chief man at their head. As they bent over Deane they began to chant a low monotone which awakened little Isobel, who sat up and stared sleepily at the strange scene. Billy went to her and gathered her close in his arms. She was sleeping again when he put her down among the blankets. The Eskimos were gone with their burden. He could hear the low chanting of the tribe.

"I found her, and I thought she was mine," said Pelliter's low voice at his side. "But she ain't, Billy. She's yours."

MacVeigh broke in on him as though he had not heard.

"You better get to bed, Pelly," he warned. "That arm needs rest. I'm going out to see where they bury him."

He put on his cap and heavy coat and went as far as the door, then turned back. From his kit he took a belt-ax and nails.

The wind was blowing more strongly over the Barren, and MacVeigh could no longer hear the low lament of the Eskimos. He moved toward their fires, and found them deserted of men, only the dogs rema g in their deathlike sleep. And then, far down the edge of the timber, he saw a flare of light. Five minutes later he stood hidden in a deep shadow, a few paces from the Eskimos. They had dug the grave early in the evening, out on the great snow-plain, free of the trees; and as the fire they had built lighted up their dark, round faces MacVeigh saw the five little black men who had borne forth Scottie Deane leaning over the shallow hole in the frozen earth. Scottie was already gone. The earth and ice and frozen moss were falling in upon him, and not a sound fell now from the thick lips of his savage mourners. In a few minutes the crude work was done, and like a thin black shadow the natives filed back to their camp. Only one remained, sitting cross-legged at the head of the grave, his long narwhal spear at his back. It was O-gluck-gluck, the Eskimo chief, guarding the dead man from the devils who come to steal body and soul during the first few hours of burial.

Billy went deeper into the forest until he found a thin, straight sapling, which he cut down with half a dozen strokes of his belt-ax. From the sapling he stripped the bark, and then he chopped off a third of its length and nailed it crosswise to what remained. After that he sharpened the bottom end and returned to the grave, carrying the cross over his shoulder. Stripped to whiteness, it gleamed in the fire-light. The Eskimo watcher stared at it for a moment, his dull eyes burning darker in the night, for he knew that after this two gods, and not one, were to guard the grave. Billy drove the cross deep, and as the blows of his ax fell upon it the Eskimo slunk back until he was swallowed in the gloom. When MacVeigh was done he pulled off his cap. But it was not to pray.

"I'm sorry, old man," he said to what was under the cross. "God knows I'm sorry. I wish you was alive. I wish you was going back to her-- with the kid-- instid o' me. But I'll keep that promise. I swear it. I'll do-- what's right-- by her."

From the forest he looked back. The Eskimo chief had returned to his somber watch. The cross gleamed a ghostly white against the thick blackness of the Barren. He turned his face away for the last time, and there filled him the oppression of a leaden hand, a thing that was both dread and fear. Scottie Deane was dead-- dead and in his grave, and yet he walked with him now at his side. He could feel the presence, and that presence was like a warning, stirring strange thoughts within him. He turned back to the cabin and entered softly. Pelliter was asleep. Little Isobel was breathing the sweet forgetfulness of childhood. He stooped and kissed her silken curls, and for a long time he stood with one of those soft curls between his fingers. In a few years more, he thought, it would be the darker gold and brown of the woman's hair-- of the woman he loved. Slowly a great peace entered into him. After all, there was more than hope ahead for him. She-- the older Isobel-- knew that he loved her as no other man in the world could love her. He had given proof of that. And now he was going to her.

XIV
THE SNOW-MAN

A fter his return from the scene of burial Billy undressed, put out the light, and went to bed. He fell asleep quickly, and his slumber was filled with many dreams. They were sweet and joyous at first, and he lived again his first meeting with the woman; he was once more in the presence of her beauty, her purity, her faith and confidence in him. And then more trouble visions came to him. He awoke twice, and each time he sat up, filled with the shuddering dread that had come to him at the graveside.

A third time he awakened, and he struck a match to look at his watch. It was four o'clock. He was still exhausted. His limbs ached from the tremendous strain of the fifty-mile race across the Barren, but he could no longer sleep. Something-- he did not attempt to ask himself what it was-- was urging him to action. He got up and dressed.

When Pelliter awoke two hours later MacVeigh's pack and sledge were ready for the trip south. While they ate their breakfast the two men finished their plans. When the hour of parting came Billy left his comrade alone with little Isobel and went out to hitch up the dogs. When he returned there was a fresh redness in Pelliter's eyes, and he puffed out thick clouds of smoke from his pipe to hide his face. MacVeigh thought of that parting often in the days that followed. Pelliter stood last in the door, and in his face was a look which MacVeigh wished that he had not seen. In his own heart was the dread and the fear, the thing which he could not name.

For hours he could not shake off the gloom that oppressed him. He strode at the head of old Kazan, the leader, striking a course due south by compass. When he fell back for the third time to look at little Isobel he found the child buried deep in her blankets sound asleep. She did not awake until he stopped to make tea at noon. It was four o'clock when he halted again to make camp in the shelter of a clump of tall spruce. Isobel had slept most of the day. She was wide awake now, laughing at him as he dug her out of her nest.

"Give me a kiss," he demanded.

Isobel complied, putting her two little hands to his face.

"You're a-- a little peach," he cried. "There ain't been a whimper out of you all day. And now we're going to have a fire-- a big fire."

He set about his work, whistling for the first time since morning. He set up his silk Service tent, cut spruce and balsam boughs until he had them a foot deep inside, and then dragged in wood for half an hour. By that time it was dark and the big fire was softening the snow for thirty feet around. He had taken off Isobel's thick, swaddling coat, and the child's pretty face shone pink in the fireglow. The light danced red and gold in her tangled curls, and as they ate supper, both on the same blanket, Billy saw opposite him more and more of what he knew he would find in the woman. When they had finished he produced a small pocket comb and drew Isobel close up to him. One by one he smoothed the tangles out of her curls, his heart beating joyously as the silken touch of them ran through his fingers. Once he had felt that same soft touch of the woman's hair against his face. It had been an accidental caress, but he had treasured it in his memory. It seemed real again now, and the thrill of it made him place little Isobel alone again on the blanket, while he rose to his feet. He threw fresh fuel on the fire, and then he found that the warmth had softened the snow until it clung to his feet. The discovery gave him an inspiration. A warmth that was not of the fire leaped into his face, and he gathered up the softened snow, raking it into piles with a snow-shoe; and before Isobel's astonished and delighted eyes there grew into shape a snow-man almost as big as himself. He gave it arms and a head, and eyes of charred wood, and when it was done he placed his own cap on the crown of it and his pipe in its mouth. Little Isobel screamed with delight, and together, hand in hand, they danced around and around it, just as he and the other girls and boys had danced years and years ago. And when they stopped there were tears of laughter and joy in the child's eyes and a filmy mist of another sort in Billy's.

It was the snow-man that brought back to him years and years of lost hopes.

They flooded in upon him until it seemed as though the old life was the life of yesterday and waiting for him now just beyond the edge of the black forest. Long after Isobel was asleep in the tent he sat and looked at the snow-man; and more and more his heart sang with a new joy, until it seemed as though he must rise and cry out in the eagerness and hope that filled him. In the snow-man, slowly melting before the fire, there was a heart and a soul and voice. It was calling to him, urging him as nothing in the world had ever urged him before. He would go back to the old home down in God's country, to the old playmates who were men and women now. They would welcome him-- and they would welcome the woman. For he would take her. For the first time he made himself believe that she would go. And there, hand in hand, they would follow his boyhood footprints over the meadows and through the hills, and he would gather flowers for her in place of the mother that was gone, and he would tell her all the old stories of the days that were passed.

It was the snow-man!

XV
LE MORT ROUGE-- AND ISOBEL

Until late that night Billy sat beside his campfire with the snow-man. Strange and new thoughts had come to him, and among these was the wondering one asking himself why he had never built a snow-man before. When he went to bed he dreamed of the snow-man and of little Isobel; and the little girl's laughter and happiness when she saw the curious form the dissolving snow-man had taken in the heat of the fire when she awoke the following morning filled him again with those boyish visions of happiness that he had seen just ahead of him. At other times he would have told himself that he was no longer reasonable. After they had breakfasted and started on the day's journey he laughed and talked with baby Isobel, and a dozen times in the forenoon he picked her up in his arms and carried her behind the dogs.

"We're going home," he kept telling her over and over again. "We're going home-- down to mama-- mama-- mama!" He emphasized that; and each time Isobel's pretty mouth formed the word mama after him his heart leaped exultantly. By the end of that day it had become the sweetest word in the world to him. He tried mother, but his little comrade looked at him blankly, and he did not like it himself. "Mama, mama, mama," he said a hundred times that night beside their campfire, and before he tucked her away in her warm blankets he said something to her about "Now I lay me down to sleep." Isobel was too tired and sleepy to comprehend much of that. Even after she was deep in slumber and Billy sat alone smoking his pipe he whispered that sweetest word in the world to himself, and took out the tress of shining hair and gazed at it joyously in the glow of the fire. By the end of the next day little Isobel could say almost the whole of the prayer his own mother had taught him years and years and years ago, so far back that his vision of her was not that of a woman, but of an elusive and wonderful angel; and the fourth day at noon she lisped the whole of it without a word of assistance from him.

On the morning of the fifth day Billy struck the Gray Beaver, and little Isobel grew serious at the change in him. He no longer amused her, but urged the dogs along, never for an instant relaxing his vigilant quest for a sign of smoke, a trail, a blazed tree. At his heart there began to burn a suspense that was almost suffocating. In these last hours before he was to see Isobel there came the inevitable reaction within him. Gloom oppressed him where a little while before joyous anticipation had given him hope. The one terrible thought drove out all others now-- he was bringing her news of death, her husband's death. And to Isobel he knew that Deane had meant all that the world held of joy or hope-- Deane and the baby.

It was like a shock when he came suddenly upon the cabin, in the edge of a small clearing. For a moment he hesitated. Then he took Isobel in his arms and went to the door. It was slightly ajar, and after knocking upon it with his fist he thrust it open and entered.

There was no one in the room in which he found himself, but there was a stove and a fire. At the end of the room was a second door, and it opened slowly. In another moment Isobel stood there. He had never seen her as he saw her now, with the light from a window falling upon her. She was dressed in a loose gown, and her long hair fell in disheveled profusion over her shoulders and bosom. MacVeigh would have cried out her name-- he had told himself a hundred times what he would first say to her-- but what he saw in her face startled him and held him silent while their eyes met. Her cheeks were flushed. Her lips burned an unnatural red. Her eyes were glowing with strange fires. She looked at him first, and her hands clutched at her bosom, crumpling the masses of her lustrous hair. Not until she had looked into his eyes did she recognize what he carried in his arms. When he held the child out to her she sprang forward with the strangest cry he had ever heard.

"My baby!" she almost shrieked. "My baby-- my baby--"

She staggered back and sank into a chair near a table, with little Isobel clasped to her breast. For a time Billy heard only those words in her dry, sobbing voice as she crushed her burning face down against her child's. He knew that she was sick, that it was fever which had sent the hot flush into her cheeks. He gulped hard, and went near to her. Trembling, he put out a hand and touched her. She looked up. A bit of that old, glorious light leaped into her eyes, the light which he had seen when in gratitude she had given him her lips to kiss.

"You?" she whispered. "You-- brought her--"

She caught his hand, and the soft smother of her loose hair fell over it. He could feel the quick rise and fall of her bosom.

"Yes," he said.

There was a demand in her face, her eyes, her parted lips. He went on, her hand clasping his tighter, until he could feel the swift beating of her heart. He had never thought that he could tell the story in as few words as he told it now, with more and more of the glorious light creeping into Isobel's eyes. She stopped breathing when he told her of the fight in the cabin and the death of the man who had stolen little Isobel. A hundred words more brought him to the edge of the forest. He stopped there. But she still questioned him in silence. She drew him down nearer, until he could feel her breath. There was something terrible in the demand of her eyes. He tried to find words to say, but something rose up in his throat and choked him. She saw his effort.

"Go on," she said, softly.

"And then-- I brought her to you," he said.

"You met him?"

Her question was so sudden that it startled him, and in an instant he had betrayed himself.

Little Isobel slipped to the floor, and Isobel stood up. She came near to him, as she came that marvelous night out on the Barren, and in her eyes there was the same prayer as she put her two hands up to him and looked straight into his face.

He thought it would be easier. But it was terrible. She did not move. No sound came from her tight-drawn lips as he told her of the meeting with Deane, and of her husband's illness. She guessed what was coming before he had spoken it. At his words, telling of death, she drew away from him slowly. She did not cry out. Her only evidence that she had heard and understood was the low moan that fell from her lips. She covered her face with her hands and stood for a moment an arm's length away, and in that moment all the force of his great love for her swept upon MacVeigh in an overwhelming flood. He opened his arms, longing to gather her into them and comfort her as he would have comforted a little child. In that love he would willingly have dropped dead at her feet if he could have given back to her the man she had lost. She raised her head in time to see his outstretched arms, she saw the love and the pleading in his face, and into her own eyes there leaped the fire of a tigress.

"You-- you--" she cried. "It was you who killed him! He had done no wrong-- save to protect me and avenge me from the insult of a brute! He had done no wrong. But the Law-- your Law-- set you after him, and you hunted him like a beast; you drove him from our home, from me and the baby. You hunted him until he died up there-- alone. You-- you killed him."

With a sudden cry she turned and caught up little Isobel and ran toward the other door. And as she disappeared into the room from which she had first appeared Billy heard her moaning those terrible words.

"You-- you-- you--"

Like a man who had been struck a blow he swayed back to the outer door. Near his dogs and sledge he met Pierre Couchée and his half-French wife coming in from their trap line. He scarcely knew what explanation he gave to the half-breed, who helped him to put up his tent. But when the latter left to follow his wife into the cabin he said:

"She ess seek, ver' seek. An' she grow more seek each day until-- mon Dieu!-- my wife, she ess scare!"

He cut a few balsam boughs and spread out his blankets, but did not trouble to build a fire. When the half-breed returned to say that supper was waiting he told him that he was not hungry, and that he was going to sleep. He doubled himself up under his blankets, silent and staring, even neglecting to feed the dogs. He was awake when the stars appeared. He was awake when the moon rose. He was still awake when the light went out in Pierre Couchée's cabin. The snow-man was gone from his vision-- home and hope. He had never been hurt as he was hurt now. He was yet awake when the moon passed far over his head, sank behind the wilderness to the west, and blackness came. Toward dawn he fell into an uneasy slumber, and from that sleep he was awakened by Pierre Couchée's voice.

When he opened his eyes it was day, and the half-breed stood at the opening of the tent. His face was filled with horror. His voice was almost a scream when he saw that MacVeigh was awake and sitting up.

"The great God in heaven!" he cried. "It is the plague, m'sieur-- le mort rouge-- the small pox! She is dying--"

MacVeigh was on his feet, gripping him by the arms.

He turned and ran toward the cabin, and Billy saw that the half-breed's team was harnessed, and that Pierre's wife was bringing forth blankets and bundles. He did not wait to question them, but hurried into the plague-stricken cabin. From the woman's room came a low moaning, and he rushed in and fell upon his knees at her side. Her face was flushed with the fever, half hidden in the disheveled masses of her hair. She recognized him, and her dark eyes burned madly.

"Take-- the baby!" she panted. "My God-- go-- go with her!"

Tenderly he put out a hand and stroked back her hair from her face.

"You are sick-- sick with the bad fever," he said, gently.

"Yes-- yes, it is that. I did not think-- until last night-- what it might be. You-- you love me! Then take her-- take the baby and go-- go-- go!"

All his old strength came back to him now. He felt no fear. He smiled down into her face, and the silken touch of her hair set his heart leaping and the love into his eyes.

"I will take her out there," he said. "But she is all right-- Isobel." He spoke her name almost pleadingly. "She is all right. She will not take the fever."

He picked up the child and carried her out into the larger room. Pierre and his wife were at the door. They were dressed for travel, as he had seen them come in off the trap line the evening before. He dropped Isobel and sprang in front of them.

"What do you mean?" he demanded. "You are not going away! You cannot go!" He turned almost fiercely upon the woman. "She will die-- if you do not stay and care for her. You shall not run away!"

"It is the plague," said Pierre. "It is death to remain!"

"You shall stay!" said MacVeigh, still speaking to Pierre's wife. "You are the one woman-- the only woman-- within a hundred miles. She will die without you. You shall stay if I have to tie you!"

With the quickness of a cat Pierre raised the butt of the heavy dog-whip which he held in his hand and it came down with a sickening thud on Billy's head. As he staggered into the middle of the cabin floor, groping blindly for a moment before he fell, he heard a strange, terrified cry, and in the open inner door he saw the white-robed figure of Isobel Deane. Then he sank down into a pit of blackness.

It was Isobel's face that he first saw when he came from out of that black pit. He knew that it was her voice calling to him before he had opened his eyes. He felt the touch of her hands, and when he looked up her loose, soft hair swept his breast. His head was bolstered up, and so he could look straight into her face. It frightened him. He knew now what she had been saying to him as he lay there upon the floor.

"You must get up! You must go!" he heard her mooning. "You must take my baby away. And you-- you-- must go!"

He pulled himself half erect, then rose to his feet, swaying a little. He came to her then, with the look in his face she had first seen out on the Barren when he had told her that he was going with her through the forest.

"No, I am not going away," he said, firmly, and yet with that same old gentleness in his voice. "If I go you will die. So I am going to stay."

She stared at him, speechless.

"You-- you can't," she gasped, at last. "Don't you see-- don't you understand? I'm a woman-- and you can't. You must take her-- my baby-- and go for help."

"There is no help," said MacVeigh, quietly. "Within a few hours you will be helpless. I am going to stay and-- and-- I swear to God I will care for you-- as he-- would have done. He made me promise that-- to care for you-- to stick by you--"

She looked straight into his eyes. He saw the twitching of her throat, the quiver of her lips. In another moment she would have fallen if he had not put a supporting arm about her.

"If-- anything-- happens," she gasped, brokenly, "you will take care-- of her-- my baby--"

"Yes-- always."

"And if I-- get well--"

Her head swayed dizzily and dropped to his breast.

"If I get-- well--"

"Yes," he urged. "Yes--"

"If I--"

He saw her struggle and fail.

"Yes, I know-- I understand," he cried, quickly, as she grew heavier in his arms. "If you get well I will go. I swear to do that. I will go away. No one will ever know--

no one in the whole world. And I will be good to you and care for you "

He stopped, brushed back her hair, and looked into her face. Then he carried her into the inner room; and when he came out little Isobel was crying.

"You poor little kid," he cried, and caught her up in his arms. "You poor little--"

The child smiled at him through her tears, and Billy suddenly sat down on the edge of the table.

"You've been a little brick from the beginning, and you're going to keep it up, little one," he said, taking her pretty face between his two big hands. "You've got to be good, for we're going to have a-- a--" He turned away, and finished under his breath. "We're going to have a devil of a time !"

XVI
THE LAW-- MURDERER OF MEN

Seated on the table, little Isobel looked up into Billy's face and laughed, and when the laugh ended in a half wail Billy found that his fingers had tightened on her little shoulder until they hurt. He tousled her hair to bring back her good-humor, and put her on the floor. Then he went back to the partly open door. It was quiet in the darkened room. He listened for a breath or a sob, and could hear neither. A curtain was drawn over the one window, and he could but indistinctly make out the darker shadow where Isobel lay on the bed. His heart beat faster as he softly called Isobel's name. There was no answer. He looked back. Little Isobel had found something on the floor and was amusing herself with it. Again he called the mother, and still there was no answer. He was filled with a sort of horror. He wanted to go over to the dark shadow and assure himself that she was breathing, but a hand seemed to thrust him back. And then, piercing him like a knife, there came again those low, moaning words of accusation:

"It was you-- it was you-- it was you--"

In that voice, low and moaning as it was, he recognized some of Pelliter's madness. It was the fever. He fell back a step and drew a hand across his forehead. It was damp, clammy with a cold perspiration. He felt a burning pain where he had been struck, and a momentary dizziness made him stagger. Then, with a tremendous effort, he threw himself together and turned to the little girl. As he carried her out through the door into the fresh air Isobel's feverish words still followed him:

"It was you-- you-- you-- you!"

The cold air did him good, and he hurried toward the tent with baby Isobel. As he deposited her among the blankets and bearskins the hopelessness of his position impressed itself swiftly upon him. The child could not remain in the cabin, and yet she would not be immune from danger in the tent, for he would have to spend a part of his time with her. He shuddered as he thought of what it might mean. For himself he had no fear of the dread disease that had stricken Isobel. He had run the risk of contagion several times before and had remained unscathed, but his soul trembled with fear as he looked into little Isobel's bright blue eyes and tenderly caressed the soft curls about her face, If Couchée and his wife had only taken her! At thought of them he sprang suddenly to his feet.

"Looky, little one, you've got to stay here!" he commanded. "Understand? I'm going to pin down the tent-flap, and you mustn't cry. If I don't get that damned half-breed, dead or alive, my name ain't Billy MacVeigh."

He fastened the tent-flap so that Isobel could not escape, and left her alone, quiet and wondering. Loneliness was not new to her. Solitude did not frighten her; and, listening with his ear close to the canvas, Billy soon heard her playing with the armful of things he had scattered about her. He hurried to the dogs and harnessed them to the sledge. Couchée and his wife did not have over half an hour the start of him-- three-quarters at the most. He would run the race of his life for an hour or two, overtake them, and bring them back at the point of his revolver. If there had to be a fight he would fight.

Where the trail struck into the forest he hesitated, wondering if he would not make better speed by leaving the team and sledge behind. The excited actions of the dogs decided him. They were sniffing at the scent left in the snow by the rival huskies, and were waiting eagerly for the command to pursue. Billy snapped his whip over their heads.

"You want a fight, do you, boys?" he cried. "So do I. Get on with you! M'hoosh! M'hoosh!"

Billy dropped upon his knees on the sledge as the dogs leaped ahead. They needed no guidance, but followed swiftly in Couchée's trail. Five minutes later they broke into thin timber, and then came out into a narrow plain, dotted with stunted scrub, through which ran the Beaver. Here the snow was soft and drifted, and Billy ran behind, hanging to the tail-rope to keep the sledge from leaving him if the dogs should develop an unexpected spurt. He could see that Couchée was exerting every effort to place distance between himself and the plague-stricken cabin, and it suddenly struck Billy that something besides fear of le mort rouge was adding speed to his heels. It was evident that the half-breed was spurred on by the thought of the blow he had struck in the cabin. Possibly he believed that he was a murderer, and Billy smiled as he observed where Couchée had whipped his dogs at a run through the soft drifts. He brought his own team down to a walk, convinced that the half-breed had lost his head, and that he would bush himself and his dogs within a few miles. He was confident, now that he would overtake them somewhere on the plain.

With the elation of this thought there came again the sudden, sickening pain in his head. It was over in an instant, but in that moment the snow had turned black, and he had flung out his arms to keep himself from falling. The babiche rope had slipped from his hand, and when things cleared before his eyes again the sledge was twenty yards ahead of him. He overtook it, and dropped upon it, panting as though he had run a race. He laughed as he recovered himself, and looked over the gray backs of the tugging dogs, but in the same breath the laugh was cut short on his lips. It was as if a knife-blade had run in one lightning thrust from the back of his neck to his brain, and he fell forward on his face with a cry of pain. After all, Couchée's blow had done the work. He realized that, and made an effort to call the dogs to a stop. For five minutes they went on, unheeding the half-dozen weak commands that he called out from the darkness that had fallen thickly about him. When at last he pulled himself up from his face and the snow turned white again, the dogs had halted. They were tangled in their traces and sniffing at the snow.

Billy sat up. Darkness and pain left him as swiftly as they had come. He saw Couchée's trail ahead, and then he looked at the dogs. They had swung at right angles to the sledge and had pulled the nose of it deep into a drift. With a sharp cry of command he sent the lash of his whip among them and went to the leader's head. The dogs slunk to their bellies, snarling at him.

"What the devil--" he began, and stopped.

He stared at the snow. Straight out from Couchée's trail there ran another-- a snow-shoe trail. For a moment he thought that Couchée or his wife had for some reason struck out a distance from their sledge. A second glance assured him that in this supposition he was wrong. Both the half-breed and his wife wore the long, narrow "bush" snow-shoes, and this second trail was made by the big, basket-shaped shoes worn by Indians and trappers on the Barrens. In addition to this, the trail was well beaten. Whoever had traveled it recently had gone over it many times before, and Billy gave utterance to his joy in a low cry. He had struck a trap line. The trapper's cabin could not be far away, and the trapper himself had passed that way not many minutes since. He examined the two trails and found where the blunt, round point of a snow-shoe had covered an imprint left by Couchée, and at this discovery Billy made a megaphone of his mittened hands and gave utterance to the long, wailing holloa of the forest man. It was a cry that would carry a mile. Twice he shouted, and the second time there came a reply. It was not far distant, and he responded with a third and still louder shout. In a flash there came again the terrible pain in his head, and he sank down on the sledge. This time he was roused from his stupor by the barking and snarling of the dogs and the voice of a man. When he lifted his head out of his arms he saw some one close to the dogs. He made an effort to rise, and staggered half to his feet. Then he fell back, and the darkness closed in about him more thickly than before. When he opened his eyes again he was in a cabin. He was conscious of warmth. The first sound that he heard was the crackling of a fire and the closing of a stove door. And then he heard some one say:

"S'help me God, if it ain't Billy MacVeigh!"

He stared up into the face that was looking down at him. It was a white man's face, covered with a scrubby red beard. The beard was new, but the eyes and the voice he would have recognized anywhere. For two years he had messed with Rookie McTabb down at Norway and Nelson House. McTabb had quit the Service because of a bad leg.

"Rookie!" he gasped.

He drew himself up, and McTabb's hands grasped his shoulders.

"S'help me, if it ain't Billy MacVeigh!" he exclaimed again, amazement in his voice and face. "Joe brought you in five minutes ago, and I ain't had a straight squint at you until now. Billy MacVeigh! Well, I'm--" He stopped to stare at Billy's forehead, where there was a stain of blood. "Hurt?" he demanded, sharply. "Was it that damned half-breed?"

Billy was gripping his hands now. Over near the stove, still kneeling before the closed door, he saw the dark face of an Indian turned toward him.

"It was Couchée," he said. "He hit me with the butt of his whip, and I've had funny spells ever since. Before I have another I want to tell you what I'm up against,

Rookie. My Gawd, it's a funny chance that ran me up against you-- just in time! Listen."

He told McTabb briefly of Scottie Deane's death, of Couchée's flight from the cabin, and the present situation there.

"There isn't a minute to lose," he finished, tightening his hold on McTabb's hand. "There's the kid and the mother, and I've got to get back to them, Rookie. The rest is up to you. We've got to get a woman. If we don't-- soon--"

He rose to his feet and stood there looking at McTabb. The other nodded.

"I understand," he said. "You're in a bad fix, Billy. It's two hundred miles to the nearest white woman, away over near Du Brochet. You couldn't get an Indian to go within half a mile of a cabin that's struck by the plague, and I doubt if this white woman would come. The only game I can see is to send to Fort Churchill or Nelson House and have the force send up a nurse. It will take two weeks."

Billy gave a gesture of despair. Indian Joe had listened attentively, and now rose quietly from his position in front of the stove.

"There's Indian camp over on Arrow Lake," he said, facing Billy. "I know squaw there who not afraid of plague."

"Sure as fate!" cried McTabb, exultantly. "Joe's mother is over there, and if there is anything on earth she won't do for Joe I can't guess what it is. Early this winter she came a hundred and fifty miles-- alone-- to pay him a visit. She'll come. Go after her, Joe. I'll go Billy MacVeigh's bond to get the Service to pay her five dollars a day from the hour she starts!" He turned to Billy. "How's your head?" he asked.

"Better. It was the run that fixed me, I guess."

"Then we'll go over to Couchée's cabin and I'll bring back the kid."

They left Joe preparing for his three-day trip into the south and east, and outside the cabin McTabb insisted on Billy riding behind the dogs. They struck back for Couchée's trail, and when they came to it McTabb laughed.

"I'll bet they're running like rabbits," he said. "What in thunder did you expect to do if you caught 'em, Billy? Drag the woman back by the hair of 'er 'ead? I'm glad you tumbled where you did. You've got to beat a lynx to beat Couchée. He'd have perforated you from behind a snow-drift sure as your name's Billy MacVeigh."

Billy felt that an immense load had been lifted from him, and he was partly inclined to tell his companion more about Isobel and himself. This, however, he did not do. As McTabb strode ahead and urged on the dogs he figured on the chances of Joe and his mother returning within a week. During that time he would be alone with Isobel, and in spite of the horrible fear that never for a moment left his heart it was impossible for him not to feel a thrill of pleasure at the thought. Those would be days of agony for himself as well as for her, and yet he would be near, always near, the woman he loved. And little Isobel would be safe in Rookie's cabin. If anything happened--

His hands gripped the edges of the sledge at the thought that leaped into his brain. It was Pelliter's thought. If anything happened to Isobel the little girl would be his own, forever and forever. He thrust the thought from him as if it were the plague itself. Isobel would live. He would make her live, If she died--

McTabb heard the low cry that broke from his lips. He could not keep it back. Good God, if she went, how empty the world would be! He might never see her again after these days of terror that were ahead of him; but if she lived, and he knew that the sun was shining in her bright hair, and that her blue eyes still looked up at the stars, and that in her sweet prayers she sometimes thought of him-- along with Deane-- life could not be quite so lonely for him.

McTabb had dropped back to his side.

"Head hurt?" he asked.

"A little," lied Billy. "There's a level stretch ahead, Rookie. Hustle up the dogs!"

Half an hour later the sledge drew up in front of Couchée's cabin. Billy pointed to the tent.

"The little one is in there," he said. "Go over an' get acquainted, Rookie. I'm going to take a look inside to see if everything is all right."

He entered the cabin quietly and closed the door softly behind him. The inner door was as he had left it, partly open, and he looked in, with a wildly beating heart. He could no longer hesitate. He stepped in and spoke her name.

"Isobel!"

There was a movement on the bed, and he was startled by the suddenness with which Isobel sprang to her feet. She drew aside the heavy curtain from the window and stood in the light. For a moment Billy saw her blue eyes filled with a strange fire as she stared at him. There was a wild flush in her cheeks, and he could hear her dry breath as it came from between her parted lips. Her hair was still undone and covered her in a shimmering veil.

"I've found a trapper's cabin, Isobel, and we're taking the baby there," he went on. "She will be safe. And we're sending for help-- for a woman--"

He stopped, horror striking him dumb. He saw more plainly the feverish madness in Isobel's eyes. She dropped the curtain, and they were in gloom. The whispered words he heard were more terrible than the madness in her eyes.

"You won't kill her?" she pleaded. "You won't kill my baby? You won't kill her--"

She staggered, back toward the bed, whispering the words over and over again. Not until she had dropped upon it did Billy move. The blood in his body seemed to have turned cold. Be dropped upon his knees at her side. His hand buried itself in the soft smother of her hair, but he no longer felt the touch of it. He tried to speak, but words would not come. And then, suddenly, she thrust him back, and he could see the glow of her eyes in the half darkness. For a moment she seemed to have fought herself out of her delirium.

"It was you-- you-- who helped to kill him!" she panted. "It was the Law-- and you are the Law. It kills-- kills-- kills-- and it never gives back when it makes a mistake. He was innocent, but you and the Law hounded him until he died. You are the murderers. You killed him. You have killed me. And you will never be punished-- never-- never-- because you are the Law-- and because the Law can kill-- kill-- kill--"

She dropped back, moaning, and MacVeigh crouched at her side, his fingers buried in her hair, with no words to say. In a moment she breathed easier. He felt her tense body relax. He forced himself to his feet and dragged himself into the outer room, closing the door after him. Even in her delirium Isobel had spoken the truth. Forever she had digged for him a black abyss between them. The Law had killed Scottie Deane. And he was the Law. And for the Law there was no punishment, even though it took the life of an innocent man. He went outside. McTabb was in the tent. The gloom of evening was closing in on a desolate world. Overhead the sky was thick, and suddenly, with a great cry, Billy flung his arms straight up over his head and cursed that Law which could not be punished, the Law that had killed Scottie Deane. For he was that Law, and Isobel had called him a murderer.

XVII
ISOBEL FACES THE ABYSS

It was not the face of MacVeigh-- the old MacVeigh-- that Rookie McTabb, the ex-constable, looked into a few moments later. Days of sickness could have laid no heavier hand upon him than had those few minutes in the darkened room of the cabin. His face was white and drawn. There were tense lines at the corners of his mouth and something strange and disquieting in his eyes. McTabb did not see the change until he came out into what remained of the day with little Isobel in his arms. Then he stared.

"That blow got you bad," he said. "You look sick. Mebbe I'd better stay with you here to-night."

"No, you hadn't," replied Billy, trying to throw off what he knew the other saw. "Take the kid over to the cabin. A night's sleep and I'll be as lively as a cat. I'm going to vaccinate her before you go."

He went into the tent and dug out from his pack the small rubber pouch in which he carried a few medicines and a roll of medicated cotton. In a small bottle there were three vaccine points. He returned with these and the cotton.

"Watch her close," he said, as he rolled back the child's sleeve. "I'm going to give you an extra point, and if this doesn't work by the seventh or eighth day you must do the job over again."

With the point of his knife he began to work gently on baby Isobel's tender pink skin. He had expected that she would cry. But she was not frightened, and her big blue eyes followed his movements wonderingly. At last it began to hurt, and her lips quivered. But she made no sound, and as tears welled into her eyes Billy dropped his knife and caught her up close to his breast.

"God bless your dear little heart," he cried, smothering his face in her silken curls. "You've been hurt so much, an' you've froze, an' you've starved, an' you ain't never said a word about it since that day up at Fullerton! Little sweetheart--"

McTabb heard him whispering things, and little Isobel's arms crept tightly about his neck. After a little Billy held her out to him again, and a part of what Rookie had seen in his face was gone.

"It won't hurt any more," he said, as he rubbed the vaccine point over the red spot on her arm. "You don't want to be sick, do you? And that 'll keep you from being sick. There--"

He wound a strip of the cotton about her arm, tied it, and gave part of what remained to McTabb. Then he took her in his arms again and kissed her warm face and her soft curls, and after that bundled her in furs and put her on the sledge. Rookie was straightening out the dogs when, like a thief, he clipped off one of the curls with his knife. Isobel laughed gleefully when she saw the curl between his fingers. Before McTabb had turned it was in his pocket.

"I won't see her again-- soon," MacVeigh said; and he tried to keep a thickness out of his voice. "That is, I-- I won't see her to-- to handle her. I'll come over now and then an' look at her from the edge of the woods. You bring 'er out, Rookie, an' don't you dare to let her know I'm out there. She wouldn't know what it meant if I didn't come to her."

He watched them as they disappeared into the gloom of night, and when they had gone a groan of anguish broke from his lips. For he knew that little Isobel was going from him forever. He would see her again-- from the edge of the forest; but he would never hold her in his arms, nor feel again her tender arms about his neck or the soft smother of her hair against his face. Long before the dread menace of the plague was lifted from the cabin and from himself he would be gone. For that was what Isobel, the mother, had demanded, and he would keep his promise to her. She would never know what happened in these days of her delirium. She would not have to face him afterward. He knew already how he would go. When help came he would slip away quietly some night, and the big wilderness would swallow him up. His plans seemed to come without thought on his own part. He would go to Fort Churchill and testify against Bucky Smith. And then he would quit the Service. His term of enlistment expired in a month, and he would not re-enlist. "It was the Law that killed him-- and you are the Law. It kills-- kills-- kills-- and it never gives back when it makes a mistake." Under the dark sky those words seemed never to end in his ears, and each moment they added to his hatred of the thing of which he had been a part for years. He seemed to hear Isobel's accusing voice in the low soughing of the night wind in the spruce tops; and in the stillness of the world that hung heavy and close about him the words chased each other through his brain until they seemed to leave behind them a path of fire.

"It kills-- kills-- kills-- and it never gives back when it makes a mistake."

His lips were set tensely as he faced the cabin. He remembered now more than one instance where the Law had killed and had never given back. That was a part of the game of man-hunting. But he had never thought of it in Isobel's way until she had painted for him in those few half-mad, accusing words a picture of himself. The fact that he had fought for Scottie Deane and had given him his freedom did not exonerate himself in his own eyes now. It was because of himself and Pelliter chiefly that Deane and Isobel had been forced to seek refuge among the Eskimos. From Fullerton they had watched and hunted for him as they would have hunted for an animal. He saw himself as Isobel must see him now-- the murderer of her husband. He was glad, as he returned to the cabin, that he had happened to come in the second or third day of her fever. He dreaded her sanity now more than her delirium,

He lighted a tin lamp in the cabin and listened for a moment at the inner door. Isobel was quiet. For the first time he made a more careful note of the cabin. Couchée and his wife had left plenty of food. He had noticed a frozen haunch of venison hanging outside the cabin, and he went out and chopped off several pieces of the meat. He did not feel hungry enough to prepare food for himself, but put the meat in a pot and placed it on the stove, that he might have broth for Isobel.

He began to find signs of her presence in the room as he moved about. Hanging on a wooden peg in the log wall he saw a scarf which he knew belonged to her. Under the scarf there was a pair of her shoes, and then he noticed that the crude cabin table was covered with a litter of stuff which he had not observed before. There were needles and thread, some cloth, a pair of gloves, and a red bow of ribbon which Isobel had worn at her throat. What held his eyes were two bundles of old letters tied with blue ribbon, and a third pile, undone and scattered. In the light of the lamp he saw that all of the writing on the envelopes was in the same hand. The top envelope on the first pile was addressed to "Mrs. Isobel Deane, Prince Albert, Saskatchewan"; the first envelope of the other bundle to "Miss Isobel Rowland, Montreal, Canada." Billy's heart choked him as he gathered the loose letters in his hands and placed them, with the others, on a little shelf above the table. He knew that they were letters from Deane, and that in her fever and loneliness Isobel had been reading them when he brought to her news of her husband's death.

He was about to remove the other articles from the table where a folded newspaper clipping was uncovered by the removal of the cloth. It was a half page from a Montreal daily, and out of it there looked straight up at him the face of Isobel Deane. It was a younger, more girlish-looking face, but to him it was not half so beautiful as the face of the Isobel who had come to him from out of the Barren. His fingers trembled and his breath came more quickly as he held the paper in the light and read the few lines under the picture:

ISOBEL ROWLAND, ONE OF THE LAST OF MONTREAL'S DAUGHTERS OF THE

NORTH, WHO HAS SACRIFICED A FORTUNE FOR LOVE OF A YOUNG ENGINEER

In spite of the feeling of shame that crept over him at thus allowing himself to be drawn into a past sacred to Isobel and the man who had died, Billy's eyes sought the date-line. The paper was eight years old. And then he read what followed. In those few minutes, as the cold, black type revealed to him the story of Isobel and Deane, he forgot that he was in the cabin, and that he could almost hear the breathing of the woman whose sweet romance had ended now in tragedy. He was with Deane that day, years ago, when he had first looked into Isobel's eyes in the little old cemetery of nameless and savage dead at Ste. Anne de Beaupré; he heard the tolling of the ancient bell in the church that had stood on the hillside for more than two hundred and fifty years; and he could hear Deane's voice as he told Isobel the story of that bell and how, in the days of old, it had often called the settlers in to fight against the Indians. And then, as he read on, he could feel the sudden thrill in Deane's blood when Isobel had told him who she was, and that Pierre Radisson, one of the great lords of the north, had been her great-grandfather; that he had brought offerings to the little old church, and that he had fought there and died close by, and that his body was somewhere among the nameless and unmarked dead. It was a beautiful story, and MacVeigh saw more of it between the lines than could ever have been printed. Once he had gone to Ste. Anne de Beaupré to see the pilgrims and the miracles there, and there flashed before him the sunlit slope overlooking the broad St. Lawrence, where Isobel and Deane had afterward met, and where she had told him how large a part the little old cracked bell, the ancient church, and the plot of nameless dead had played in her life ever since she could remember. His blood grew hot as he read of what followed the beginning of love at the pilgrims' shrine. Isobel had no father or mother, the paper said. Her uncle and guardian was an iron master of the old blood-- the blood that had been a part of the wilderness and the great company since the day the first "gentlemen adventurers" came over with Prince Rupert. He lived alone with Isobel in a big white house on the top of a hill, shut in by stone walls and iron pickets, and looked out upon the world with the cold hauteur of a feudal lord. He was young David Deane's enemy from the moment he first heard about him, largely because he was nothing more than a struggling mining engineer, but chiefly because he was an American and had come from across the border. The stone walls and iron pickets were made a barrier to him. The heavy gates never opened for him. Then had come the break. Isobel, loyal in her love, had gone to Deane. The story ended there.

For a few moments Billy stood with the paper in his hand, the type a blur before his eyes. He could almost see Isobel's old home in Montreal. It was on the steep, shaded road leading up to Mount Royal, where he had once watched a string of horses "tacking" with their two-wheeled carts of coal in their arduous journey to Sir George Allen's basement at the end of it. He remembered how that street had held a curious sort of fascination for him, with its massive stone walls, its old French homes, and that old atmosphere still clinging to it of the Montreal of a hundred years ago. Twelve years before he had gone there first and carved his name on the wooden stairway leading to the top of the mountain. Isobel had been there then. Perhaps it was she he had heard singing behind one of the walls.

He put the paper with the letters, making a note of the uncle's name. If anything happened it would be his duty to send word to him-- perhaps. And then, deliberately, he tore into little pieces the slip of paper on which he had written the name. Geoffrey Renaud had cast off his niece. And if she died why should he-- Billy MacVeigh-- tell him anything about little Isobel? Since Isobel's terrible castigation of himself and the Law duty had begun to hold a diferent meaning for him.

Several times during the next hour Billy listened at the door. Then he made some tea and toast and took the broth from the stove. He went into the room, leaving these on the hearth of the stove so that they would not grow cold. He heard Isobel move, and as he went to her side she gave a little breathless cry.

"David-- David-- is it you?" she moaned. "Oh, David, I'm so glad you have come!"

Billy stood over her. In the darkness his face was ashen gray, for like a flash of fire in the lightless room the truth rushed upon him. Shock and fever had done their work. And in her delirium Isobel believed that he was Deane, her husband. In the gloom he saw that she was reaching up her arms to him.

"David!" she whispered; and in her voice there were a love and gladness that thrilled and terrified him to the quick of his soul.

XVIII
THE FULFILMENT OF A PROMISE

In the space of silence that followed Isobel's whispered words there came to Billy a realization of the crisis which he faced. The thought of surrendering himself to his first impulse, and of taking Deane's place in these hours of Isobel's fever, filled him instantly with a revulsion that sent him back a step from the bed, his hands clenched until his nails hurt his calloused palms.

"No, no, I am not David," he began, but the words died in his throat.

To tell her that, to make her know the truth-- that her husband was dead-- might kill her now. Hope, belief that he was alive and with her, would help to make her live. So quickly that he could not have spoken his thoughts in words these things flashed upon him. If Deane were alive and at her side his presence would save her. And if she believed that he was Deane he would save her. In the end she would never know. He remembered how Pelliter had forgotten things that had happened in his delirium. To Isobel, when she awakened into sanity, it would only seem like a dream at most. A few words from him then would convince her of that. If necessary, he would tell her that she had talked much about David in her fever and had imagined him with her. She would have no suspicion that he had played that part.

Isobel had waited a moment, but now she whispered again, as if a little frightened at his silence.

"David-- David--"

He stepped back quickly to the bed and his hands met those reaching up to him. They were hot and dry, and Isobel's fingers tightened about his own almost fiercely, and drew his hands down on her breast. She gave a sigh, as though she would rest easier now that his hands were touching her.

"I have been making some broth for you," he said, scarcely daring to speak. "Will you take some of it, Isobel? You must-- and sleep."

He felt the pressure of Isobel's hands, and she spoke to him so calmly that for a breath he thought that she must surely be herself again.

"I don't like the dark, David," she said. "I can't see you. And I want to do up my hair. Will you bring in a light?"

"Not until you are better," he whispered. "A light will hurt your eyes. I will stay with you-- near you--"

She raised a hand in the darkness, and it stroked his face. In that touch were all the love and gentleness that had lived for the man who was dead, and the caress thrilled Billy until it seemed as though what was in his heart must burst forth in a sobbing breath. Suddenly her hand left his face, and he heard her moving restlessly.

"My hair-- David--"

He put out a hand, and it fell in the soft smother of her hair. It was tangled about her face and neck, and he lifted her gently while he drew out the thick masses of it. He did not dare to speak while he smoothed out the rich tresses and pleated them into a braid. Isobel sighed restfully when he had done.

"I am going to get the broth now," he said then.

He went into the outer room where the lamp was lighted. Not until he took up the cup of broth did he notice how his hand trembled. A bit of the broth spilled on the floor, and he dropped a piece of the toast. He, too, was passing through the crucible with Isobel Deane.

He went back and lifted her so that her head rested against his shoulder and the warmth of her hair lay against his cheek and neck. Obediently she ate the half-dozen bits of toast he moistened in the broth, and then drank a few sips of the liquid. She would have rested there after that, with her face turned against his, and Billy knew that she would have slept. But he lowered her gently to the pillow.

"You must go to sleep now," he urged, softly. "Good night--"

"David!"

"Yes--"

"You-- you-- haven't-- kissed-- me--"

There was a childish plaint in her voice, and with a sob in his own breath he bent over her. For an instant her arms clung about his neck. He felt the sweet, thrilling touch of her warm lips, and then he drew himself back; and, with her "Good night, David" following him to the door, he went into the outer room, and with a strange, broken cry flung himself on the cot in which Couchée had slept.

It was an hour before he raised his face from the blankets. Yet he had not slept. In that hour, and in the half-hour that had preceded it in Isobel's room, there had come lines into his face which made him look older. Once Isobel had kissed him, and he had treasured that kiss as the sweetest thing that had come to him in all his life. And to-night she had given him more than that, for there had been love, and not gratitude alone, in the warmth of her lips, in the caress of her hands and arms, and in the pressure of her feverish face against his own. But they brought him none of the pleasure of that which she had given to him on the Barren. Grief-stricken, he rose and faced the door. In spite of the fact that he knew there was no alternative for him, he regarded himself as worse than a thief. He was taking an advantage of her which filled him with a repugnance for himself, and he prayed for the hour when sanity would return to her, though it brought back the heartbreak and despair that were now lost in the oblivion of her fever. Always in the northland there is somewhere the dread trail of le mort rouge, the "red death," and he was well acquainted with the course it would have to run. He believed that the fever had stricken Isobel the third or fourth day before, and there would follow three or four days more in which she would not be herself. Then would come the reaction. She would awaken to the truth then that her husband was dead, and that he had been with her alone all that time.

He listened for a moment at the door. Isobel was resting quietly, and he went out of the cabin without making a sound. The night had grown blacker and gloomier. There was not a rift in the sullen darkness of the sky over him. A wind had risen from out of the north and east, just enough of a wind to set the tree-tops moaning and fill the closed-in world about him with uneasy sound. He walked toward the tent where little Isobel had been, and there was something in the air that choked him. He wished that he had not sent all of the dogs with McTabb. A terrible loneliness oppressed him. It was like a clammy hand smothering his heart in its grip, and it made him sick. He turned and looked at the light in the cabin. Isobel was there, and he had thought that where she was he could never be lonely. But he knew now that there lay between them a gulf which an eternity could not bridge.

He shuddered, for with the night wind it seemed to him that there came again the presence of Scottie Deane. He gripped his hands and stared out into a pit of blackness. It was as if he had heard the Wild Horsemen passing that way, panting and galloping through the spruce tops on their mission of gathering the souls of the dead. Deane was with him, as his spirit had been with him on that night he had returned to Pelliter after putting the cross over Scottie's grave. And in a moment or two the feeling of that presence seemed to lift the smothering weight from his heart. He knew that Deane could understand, and the presence comforted him. He went to the tent and looked in, though there was nothing to see. And then he turned back to the cabin. Thought of the grave with its sapling cross brought home to him his duty to the woman. From the rubber pouch he brought forth his pad of paper and a pencil.

For more than an hour after that he worked. steadily in the dull glow of the lamp. He knew that Isobel would return to Deane. It might be soon-- or a long time from now. But she would go. And step by step he mapped out for her the trail that led to the little cabin on the edge of the Barren. And after that he wrote in his big, rough hand what was overflowing from his heart.

"May God take care of you always. I would give my life to give you back his. I won't let his grave be lost. I will go back some day and plant blue flowers over it. I guess you will never know what I would do to give him back to you and make you happy."

He knew that he had not promised what he would fail to do. He would return to the lonely grave on the edge of the Barren. There was something that called him to it now, something that he could not understand, and which came of his own desolation. He folded the pages of paper, wrapped them in a clean sheet, and wrote Isobel Deans's name on the outside. Then he placed the packet with the letters on the shelf over the table. He knew that she would find it with them.

What happened during the terrible week that followed that night no one but MacVeigh would ever know. To him they were seven days of a fight whose memory would remain with him until the end of time. Sleepless nights and almost sleepless days. A bitter struggle, almost without rest, with the horrible specter that ever hovered within the inner room. A struggle that drew his cheeks in and put deep lines in his face; a struggle during which Isobel's voice spoke tenderly and plead-ingly with him in one hour and bitterly in the next. He felt the caress of her hands. More than once she drew him down to the soft thrill of her feverish lips. And then, in more terrible moments, she accused him of hunting to death the man who lay back under the sapling cross. The three days of torment lengthened into four, and the four into seven, To the bottom of his soul he suffered, for he understood what it all meant for him. On the third and the fifth and the seventh days he went over to McTabb's cabin, and Rookie came out and talked with him at a distance through a birchbark megaphone. On the seventh day there was still no news of Indian Joe and his mother. And on this day Billy played his last part as Deane. He went into her room at noon with broth and toast and a dish of water, and after she had eaten a little he lifted her and made a prop of blankets at her back so that he could brush out and braid her beautiful hair. It was light in the room in spite of the curtain which he kept closely drawn. Outside the sun was shining brightly, and the pale luster of it came through the curtain and lit up the rich tresses he was brushing. When he was done he lowered her gently to her pillow. She was looking at him strangely. And then, with a shock that seemed to turn him cold to the depths of his soul, he saw what was in her eyes. Sanity and reason. He saw swiftly gathering in them the old terror, the old grief-- recognition of his true self! He waited to hear no word, but turned as he had done a hundred times before and left the room.

In the outer room he stood for a few silent minutes, gathering strength for the ordeal that was near. The end was at hand-- for him. He choked back his weakness, and after a time returned to the inner door. But now he did not go in as he had en-tered before. He knocked. It was the first time. And Isobel's voice bade him enter.

His heart was filled with a sudden throbbing pain when he saw that she had turned so that she lay with her face turned away from him. He bent over her and said, softly:

"You are better. The danger is past."

"I am better and-- and-- it is over ?" he heard her whisper.

"Yes."

"The-- the baby?"

"Is well-- yes."

There was a moment's silence. The room seemed to tremble with it. Then she said, faintly:

"You have been alone?"

"Yes-- alone-- for seven days."

She turned her eyes upon him fully. He could see the glow of them in the faint light. It seemed to him that she was reading him to the depths of his soul, and that in this moment she knew! She knew that he had taken the part of David, and suddenly she turned her face away from him again with a strange, choking sob. He could feel her trembling. She seemed, struggling for breath and strength, and he heard again the words "You-- you-- you--"

"Yes, yes-- I know-- I understand," he said, and his heart choked him. "You must be quiet-- now. I promised you that if you got well I would go. And-- I will. No one will ever know. I will go."

"And you will never come to me again?" Her voice was terribly quiet and cold.

"Never," he said. "I swear that."

She had drawn away from him now until he could see nothing of her but the shimmer of her thick braid where it lay in a ray of light. But he could hear her sobbing breath. She scarcely knew when he left the room, he went so quietly. He closed her door after him, and this time he latched it. The outer door was open, and suddenly he heard that for which he had been waiting and listening-- the short, sharp yelping of dogs, and a human voice.

In three leaps he was out in the open. Halfway across the narrow clearing Indian Joe had halted with his team. One glance at the sledge showed Billy that Joe's mother had not failed him. A thin, weazened little old woman scrambled from a pile of bearskins as he ran toward them. She had sunken eyes that watched his approach with a ratlike glitter, and her naked hands were so emaciated that they looked like claws; but in spite of her unprepossessing appearance Billy almost hugged her in his delight at their coming. Maballa was her name, Rookie had told him, and she understood and could talk English better than her son. Billy told her of the condition in the cabin, and when he had finished she took a small pack from the sledge, cackled a few words to Indian Joe, and followed him without a moment's hesitation. That she had no fear of the plague added to Billy's feeling of relief. As soon as she had taken off her hood and heavy blanket she went fearlessly into the inner room, and a moment later Billy heard her talking to Isobel.

It took him but a few moments to gather up the few things he possessed and put them in his pack. Then he went out and took down his tent. Indian Joe had already gone, and he followed in his trail. An hour later McTabb appeared at the door of his cabin, summoned by Billy's shout. He circled about and came up with the wind, until he stood within fifty paces of MacVeigh. Billy told him what he was going to do. He was going to Churchill, and would leave Isobel and the baby in his care. From Fort Churchill he would send back an escort to take the woman and little Isobel down to civilization. He wanted fresh clothes-- anything he could wear. Those he had on he would be compelled to burn. He suggested that he could get into one of Indian Joe's outfits, if he had any spare garments, and McTabb went back to the cabin, returning a few minutes later with an armful of clothes.

"Here's everything you'll need, except an undershirt an' drawers," said McTabb, placing them in a pile on the snow. "I'll wait a little while you're changing. Better burn those quick. The wind might change, and I don't want to be caught in a whiff of it."

He moved to a safe distance while Billy secured the clothes and went into the timber. From a birch tree he pulled off a pile of bark, and as he stripped he put his old clothes on it. McTabb could hear the crackling and snapping of the fire when Billy reappeared arrayed in Indian Joe's "second best"-- buckskin trousers, a worn and tattered fur coat, a fisher-skin cap, and moccasins a size too small for him. For fifteen minutes the two men talked, McTabb still drawing the dead-line at fifty paces. Then he went back and brought up Billy's dogs and sledge.

"I'd like to shake hands with you, Billy," he apologized, "but I guess it's best not to. I don't suppose-- we'd dare-- bring out the kid?"

"No," said Billy. "Good-by, Mac. I'll see you-- sometime-- later. Just go back-- an' bring her to the door, will you? I don't want her to know I'm here, an' I'll take a look at her from the bush. She wouldn't understand, you know, if she knew I was here an' wouldn't come up an' see her."

He concealed himself among the spruce as McTabb went into the cabin. A moment later he reappeared. Isobel was in his arms, and Billy gulped back a sob. For an instant she turned her face his way, and he could see that she was pointing in his direction as Rookie talked to her, and then for another instant the sun lit up the child's hair with a golden fire, as he had first seen it on that wonderful day at Fullerton. He wanted to cry out one word to her-- at least one-- but what came was only the sob he had fought to keep back. He turned his face into the forest. And this time he knew that the parting was final.

XIX
A PILGRIMAGE TO THE BARREN

The fourth night after he had left the plague-stricken cabin Billy was camped on Lame Otter Creek, one hundred and eighty miles from Fort Churchill, over on Hudson's Bay. He had eaten his supper, and was smoking his pipe. It was a clear and glorious night, with the sky afire with stars and a full moon. Several times Billy had stared at the moon. It was what the Indians called "the bleeding moon"-- red as blood, with an uneven, dripping edge. It was the Indian superstition that it meant misfortune to those who did not keep it at their backs. For seven consecutive nights it had made a red trail through the skies in that terrible year of plague nineteen years before, when a quarter of the forest population of the north had died. Since then it had been known as the "plague moon." Billy had seen it only twice before. He was not superstitious, but to-night he was filled with a strange sensation of uneasiness. He laughed an unpleasant laugh as he stared into the crackling birch flames and wondered what new misfortune could come to him.

And then, slowly, something seemed to come to him from out of the wonderful night like a quieting hand to still the pain in his broken heart. At last, once more, he was home. For the wind-swept Barrens and the forest had been his home, and more than once he had told himself that life away from them would be impossible for him. More deeply than ever this thought came to him to-night. He had become a part of them and they a part of him. And as he looked up again at the red moon the sight of it no longer brought him uneasiness, but a strange sort of joy. For an hour he sat there, and the fire died down. About him the rustle and whisper of the wild closed in nearer. It was his world, and he breathed more deeply and listened. Lonely and sick at heart, he felt the life and sympathy and love of it creeping into him, grieving with him in his grief, warming him with its hope, pledging him again the eternal friendship of its trees, its mountains, and all of the wild that it held therein. A hundred times, in that strange man-play that comes of loneliness in the far north, he had given life and form to the star shadows about him, to the shadows of the tall spruce, the twisted shrub, the rocks, and even the mountains. And now it was no longer play. With each hour that passed this night, and with each day and night that followed, they became more real to MacVeigh; and the fires he built in the black gloom painted him pictures as they had never painted them before; and the trees and the rocks and the twisted shrub comforted him more and more in his loneliness, and gave to him the presence of life in their movement, in the coming and going of their shadow forms. Everywhere they were the same old friends, unvarying and changeless. The spruce shadow of to-night, nodding to him in its silent way, was the same that nodded to him last night-- a hundred nights ago; the stars were the same, the winds whispering to him in the tree-tops were the same, everything was as it was yesterday-- years ago. He knew that in these things, and in these things alone, he would always possess Isobel. She would return to civilization, and the shifting scenes of life down there would soon make her forget him-- almost. But in his world there was no change. Ten years from now he might go over their old trail and still find the charred remains of the campfire he had built for her that night beside the Barren. The wilderness would bear memory of her so long as he was a part of it; and now, as he came nearer to Churchill, he knew that he would always be a part of it.

Three weeks after he had left Couchée's cabin he came into Fort Churchill. A month had changed him so that the factor did not recognize him at first. The inspector in charge stared at him twice, and then cried, "My God, is it you, MacVeigh?" To Pelliter alone, who was waiting for him, did Billy tell all that had happened down on the Little Beaver. There were several letters waiting for him at Churchill, and one of these told him that a silver property in which he was interested over at Cobalt had turned out well and that his share in the sale was something over ten thousand dollars. He used this unexpected piece of good-fortune as an excuse to the inspector when he refused to re-enlist. A week after his arrival at Churchill Bucky Smith was dishonorably discharged from the Service. There were several near them when Bucky came up to him with a smile on his face and offered to shake hands.

"I don't bear you any ill will, Billy," he said, loud enough for the others to hear. "Only you've made a big mistake." And then, in words for Billy's ears alone, he added: "Remember what I promised you! I'll kill you for this if I have to hunt you round the world!"

A few days later Pelliter left on the last of the slush snows in an effort to reach Nelson House before the sledging was gone.

"I wish you'd go with me, Billy," he entreated for the hundredth time. "My girl 'd love to have you come, an' you know how I'd like it."

But Billy could not be moved.

"I'll come and see you some day-- when you've got the kid," he promised, trying to laugh, as he shook hands for the last time with his old comrade.

For three days after Pelliter's departure he remained at the post. On the morning of the fourth, with his pack on his back and without dogs, he struck off into the north and west.

"I think I'll spend next winter at Fond du Lac," he told the inspector. "If there's any mail for me you can send it there if you have a chance, and if I'm not at Fond du Lac it can be returned to Churchill."

He said Fond du Lac because Deane's grave lay between Churchill and the old Hudson's Bay Company's post over in the country of the Athabasca. The Barrens were the one thing that called to him now-- the one thing to which he dared respond. He would keep his promise to Isobel and visit Scottie's grave. At least he tried to make himself believe that he was keeping a promise. But deep in him there was an undercurrent of feeling which he could not explain. It was as if there were a spirit with him at times, walking at his side, and hovering about his campfire at nights, and when he gave himself up to the right mood he felt that it was the presence of Deane. He believed in strong friendship, but he had never believed in the love of man for man. He had not thought that such a thing could exist, except, perhaps, between father and son. With him, in all the castles he had built and the dreams he had dreamed, the alpha and omega of love had remained with woman. For the first time he knew what it meant to love a man-- the memory of a man.

Something held him from telling the secret of his mission at Churchill even to Pelliter. The evening before he left he had smuggled an ax into the edge of the forest, and the second day he found use for this. He came to a straight-grained, thick birch, eighteen inches in diameter, and he put up his tent fifty paces from it. Before he rolled himself in his blankets that night he had cut down the tree. The next day he chopped off the butt, and before another nightfall had hewn out a slab two inches thick, a foot wide, and three feet long. When he took up the trail into the north and west again the following morning he left the ax behind.

The fourth night he worked with his hunting-knife and his belt-ax, thinning down the slab and making it smooth. The fifth and the sixth nights he passed in the same way, and he ended the sixth night by heating the end of a small iron rod in the fire and burning the first three letters of Deane's epitaph on the slab. For a time he was puzzled, wondering whether he should use the name Scottie or David. He decided on David.

He did not travel fast, for to him spring was the most beautiful of all seasons in the wilderness. It was underfoot and overhead now. The snow-floods were singing between the ridges and gathering in the hollows. The poplar buds were swollen almost to the bursting point, and the bakneesh vines were as red as blood with the glow of new life. Seventeen days after he left Churchill he came to the edge of the big Barren. For two days he swung westward, and early in the forenoon of the third looked out over the gray waste, dotted with moving caribou, over which he and Pelliter had raced ahead of the Eskimos with little Isobel. He went to the cabin first and entered. It was evident that no one had been there since he had left, On the bunk where Deane had died he found one of baby Isobel's little mittens. He had wondered where she had lost it, and had made her a new one of lynx-skin on the way down to Couchée's cabin. The tiny bed that he had made for her on the floor was as she had last slept in it, and in the part of a blanket that he had used as a pillow was still the imprint of her head. On the wall hung a pair of old trousers that Deane had worn. Billy looked at these things, standing silently, with his pack at his feet. There was something in the cabin that closed in about him and choked him, and he struggled to overcome it by whistling. His lips seemed thick. At last he turned and went to the grave.

The foxes had been there, and had dug a little about the sapling cross. There was no other change. During the remainder of the forenoon Billy cut down a heavier sapling and sunk the butt of it three feet into the half-frozen earth at the head of Deane's grave. Then, with spikes he had brought with him, he nailed on the slab.

He believed that no one would ever know what the words on that slab meant-- no one except himself and the spirit of Scottie Deane. With the end of the heated rod he had burned into the wood:

    DAVID DEANE
    Died Feb. 27, 1908
    BELOVED OF ISOBEL AND THE ONE
    WHO WISHES HE COULD TAKE
    YOUR PLACE AND GIVE
    YOU BACK TO
    HER
    W. M. April 15, 1908

He did not stop when it was time for dinner, but carried rocks from a ridge a couple of hundred yards away, and built a cairn four feet high around the sapling, so that storm or wild animals could not knock it down. Then he began a search in the warmest and sunniest parts of the forest, where the green tips of plant life were beginning to reveal themselves. He found snowflowers, redglow, and bakneesh, and dug up root after root, and at last, peeping out from between two rocks, he found the arrowlike tip of a blue flower. The bakneesh roots he planted about the cairn, and the blue flower he planted by itself at the head of the grave.

It was long past midday when he returned to the cabin, and once more he was oppressed by the appalling loneliness of it. It was not as he had thought it would be. Deane's spirit and companionship had seemed to be nearer to him beside his camp-fires and in the forest. He cooked a meal over the stove, but the snapping of the fire seemed strange and unnatural in the deserted room. Even the air he breathed was heavy with the oppression of death and broken hopes. He found it difficult to swallow the food he had cooked, though he had eaten nothing since morning. When he was done he looked at his watch. It was four o'clock. The northern sun had dropped behind the distant forests and was followed now by the thickening gloom of early evening. For a few moments Billy stood motionless outside the cabin. Behind him an owl hooted its lonely mating-song. Over his head a brush sparrow twittered. It was that hour, just between the end of day and the beginning of night, when the wilderness holds its breath and all is still. Billy clenched his hands and listened. He could not keep back the break that was in his breath. Something out there in the silence and the gathering darkness was calling him-- calling him away from the cabin, away from the grave, and the gray, dead waste of the Barren. He turned back into the cabin and put his things into the pack. He took the little mitten to keep with his other treasures, and then he went out and closed the door behind him. He passed close to the grave and for the last time gazed upon the spot where Deane lay buried.

"Good-by, old man," he whispered. Goodby--"

The owl hooted louder as he turned his face into the west. It made him shiver, and he hurried his steps into the unbroken wilderness that lay for hundreds of miles between him and the post at Fond du Lac.

XX
THE LETTER

Days and weeks and months of a loneliness which Billy had never known before followed after his pilgrimage to Deane's grave. It was more than loneliness. He had known loneliness, the heartbreak and the longing of it, in the black and silent chaos of the arctic night; he had almost gone mad of it, and he had seen Pelliter nearly die for a glimpse of the sun and the sound of a voice. But this was different. It was something that ate deeper at his soul each day and each night that he lived. He had believed that thought of Isobel and his memories of her would make him happier, even though he never saw her again. But in this he was mistaken. The wilderness does not lend to forgetfulness, and each day her voice seemed nearer and more real to him, and she became more and more insistently a part of his thoughts. Never an hour of the day passed that he did not ask himself where she was. He hoped that she and the baby Isobel had returned to the old home in Montreal, where they would surely find friends and be cared for. And yet the dread was upon him that she had remained in the wilderness, that her love for Deane would keep her there, and that she would find a woman's work at some post between the Height of Land and the Barrens. At times there possessed him an overwhelming desire to return to McTabb's cabin and find where they had gone. But he fought against this desire as a man fights against death. He knew that once he surrendered himself to the temptation to be near her again he would lose much that he had won in his struggle during the days of plague in Couchée's cabin.

So his feet carried him steadily westward, while the invisible hands tugged at him from behind. He did not go straight to Fond du Lac, but spent nearly three weeks with a trapper whom he ran across on the Pipestone River. It was June when he struck Fond du Lac, and he remained there a month. He had more than half expected to pass the winter there, but the factor at the post proved a disagreeable acquaintance, and he did not like the country. So early in July he set out deeper into the Athabasca country to the west, followed the northern shore of the big lake, and two months later came to Fort Chippewyan, near the mouth of the Slave River.

He struck Chippewyan at a fortunate time. A government geological and map-making party was just preparing to leave for the terra incognita between the Great Slave and the Great Bear, and the three men who had come up from Ottawa urged Billy to join them. He jumped at the opportunity, and remained with them until the party returned to the Mackenzie River by the way of Fort Providence five months later. He remained at Fort Providence until late spring, and then came down to Fort Wrigley, where he had several friends in the service. Fifteen months of wandering had had their effect upon him. He could no longer resist the call of the wanderlust. It urged him from place to place, and stronger and stronger grew in him the desire to return to his old country along the shores of the big Bay far to the west. He had partly planned to join the railroad builders on the new trans-continental in the mountains of British Columbia, but in August, instead of finding himself at Edmonton or Tête Jaune Cache, he was at Prince Albert, three hundred and fifty miles to the east. From this point he struck northward with a party of company men into the Lac La Ronge country, and in October swung eastward alone through the Sissipuk and Burntwood waterways to Nelson House. He continued northward after a week's rest, and on the eighteenth of December the first of the two great storms which made the winter of 1909-10 one of the most tragic in the history of the far northern people overtook him thirty miles from York Factory. It took him five days to reach the post, where he was held up for several weeks. These were the first of those terrible weeks of famine and intense cold during which more than fifteen hundred people died in the north country. From the Barren Lands to the edge of the southern watershed the earth lay under from four to six feet of snow, and from the middle of December until late in January the temperature did not rise above forty degrees below zero, and remained for the most of the time between fifty and sixty. From all points in the wilderness reports of starvation and death came to the company's posts. Trap lines could not be followed because of the intense cold. Moose, caribou, and even the furred animals had buried themselves under the snow. Indians and half-breeds dragged themselves into the posts. Twice at York Factory Billy saw mothers who brought dead babies in their arms. One day a white trapper came in with his dogs and sledge, and on the sledge, wrapped in a bearskin, was his wife, who had died fifty miles back in the forest.

During these terrible weeks Billy found it impossible to keep Isobel and the baby Isobel out of his mind night or day. The fear grew in him that somewhere in the wilderness they were suffering as others were suffering. So obsessed did he become with the thought that he had a terrible dream one night, and in that dream baby Isobel's face appeared to him, a deathlike mask, white and cold and thinned by starvation. The vision decided him. He would go to Fort Churchill, and if McTabb had not been driven in he would go to his cabin, over on the Little Beaver, and learn what had become of Isobel and the little girl. A few days later, on the twenty-seventh day of January, there came a sudden rise in the temperature, and Billy prepared at once to take advantage of the change. A half-breed, on his way to Churchill, accompanied him, and they set out together the following morning. On the twentieth of February they arrived at Fort Churchill.

Billy went immediately to detachment headquarters. There had been several changes in two years, and there was only one of the old force to shake hands with him. His first inquiry was about McTabb and Isobel Deane. Neither was at Churchill, nor had been there since the arrival of the new officer in charge. But there was mail for Billy-- three letters. There had been half a dozen others, but they were now following up his old trails somewhere out in the wilderness. These three had been returned recently from Fond du Lac. One was from Pelliter, the fourth he had written, he said, without an answer. The "kid" had come-- a girl-- and he wondered if Billy was dead. The second letter was from his Cobalt partner.

The third he turned over several times before he opened it. It did not look much like a letter. It was torn and ragged at the edges, and was so soiled and water-stained that the address on it was only partly legible. It had been to Fond du Lac, and from there it had followed him to Fort Chippewyan. He opened it and found that the writing inside was scarcely more legible than the inscription on the envelope. The last words were quite plain, and he gave a low cry when he found that it was from Rookie McTabb.

He went close to a window and tried to make out what McTabb had written. Here and there, where water had not obliterated the writing, he could make out a line or a few words. Nearly all was gone but the last paragraph, and when Billy came to this and read the first words of it his heart seemed all at once to die within him, and he could not see. Word by word he made out the rest after that, and when he was done he turned his stony face to the white whirl of the storm outside the window, his lips as dry as though he had passed through a fever.

A part of that last paragraph was unintelligible, but enough was left to tell him what had happened in the cabin down on the Little Beaver.

McTabb had written:

"We thought she was getting well... took sick again.... did
everything... could. But it didn't do any good,... died just five
weeks to a day after you left. We buried her just behind the cabin.
God... that kid... You don't know how I got to love her, Billy....
give her up..."

McTabb had written a dozen lines after that, but all of them were a water-stained and unintelligible blur.

Billy crushed the letter in his hand. The new inspector wondered what terrible news he had received as he walked out into the blinding chaos of the storm.

XXI
THE FIGHTING SPARK

For ten minutes Billy buried himself blindly in the storm. He scarcely knew which direction he took, but at last he found himself in the shelter of the forest, and he was whispering Isobel's name over and over again to himself.

"Dead-- dead--" he moaned. "She is dead-- dead--"

And then there rushed upon him, crushing back his deeper grief, a thought of the baby Isobel. She was still with McTabb down on the Little Beaver. In the blur of the storm he read again what he could make out of Rookie's letter. Something in that last paragraph struck him with a deadly fear. "God... that kid... You, don't know how I got to love her, Billy,... give her up..."

What did it mean? What had McTabb told him in that part of the letter that was gone?

The reaction came as he put the letter back into his pocket. He walked swiftly back to the inspector's office.

"I'm going down to the Little Beaver. I'm going to start to-day," he said. "Who is there in Churchill that I can get to go with me?"

Two hours later Billy was ready to start, with an Indian as a companion. Dogs could not be had for love or money, and they set out on snowshoes with two weeks' supply of provisions, striking south and west. The remainder of that day and the next they traveled with but little rest. Each hour that passed added to Billy's mad impatience to reach McTabb's cabin.

With the morning of the third day began the second of those two terrible storms which swept over the northland in that winter of famine and death. In spite of the Indian's advice to build a permanent camp until the temperature rose again

Billy insisted on pushing ahead. The fifth night, in the wild Barren country west of the Etawney, his Indian failed to keep up the fire, and when Billy investigated he found him half dead with a strange sickness. He made the Indian's balsam shelter snow and wind proof, cut wood, and waited. The temperature continued to fall, and the cold became intense. Each day the provisions grew less, and at last the time came when Billy knew that he was standing face to face with the Great Peril. He went farther and farther from camp in his search for game. Even the brush sparrows and snow-hawks were gone. Once the thought came to him that be might take what food was left and accept the little chance that remained of saving himself. But the idea never got farther than a first thought. On the twelfth day the Indian died. It was a terrible day. There was food for another twenty-four hours.

Billy packed it, together with his blankets and a few pieces of tinware. He wondered if the Indian had died of a contagious disease. Anyway, he made up his mind to put out the warning for others if they came that way, and over the dead Indian's balsam shelter he planted a sapling, and at the end of the sapling he fastened a strip of red cotton cloth-- the plague signal of the north.

Than he struck out through the deep snows and the twisting storm, knowing that there was no more than one chance in a thousand ahead of him, and that the one chance was to keep the wind at his back.

At the end of his first day's struggle Billy built himself a camp in a bit of scrub timber which was not much more than bush. He had observed that the timber and that every tree and bush he had passed since noon was stripped and dead on the side that faced the north. He cooked and ate his last food the following day, and went on. The small timber turned to scrub, and the scrub, in time, to vast snow wastes over which the storm swept mercilessly. All this day he looked for game, for a flutter of bird life; he chewed bark, and in the afternoon got a mouthful of foxbite, which made his throat swell until he could scarcely breathe. At night he made tea, but had nothing to eat. His hunger was acute and painful. It was torture the next day-- the third-- for the process of starvation is a rapid one in this country where only the fittest survive on from four to five meals a day. He camped, built a small bush-fire at night, and slept. He almost failed to rouse himself on the morning that followed, and when he staggered to his feet and felt the cutting sting of the storm still in his face and heard the swishing wail of it over the Barren he knew that at last the hour had come when he was standing face to face with the Almighty.

For some strange reason he was not frightened at the situation. He found that even over the level spaces he could scarce drag his snow-shoes, but this had ceased to alarm him as he had been alarmed at first. He went on, hour after hour, weaker and weaker. Within himself there was still life which reasoned that if death were to come it could not come in a better way. It at least promised to be painless-- even pleasant. The sharp, stinging pains of hunger, like little electrical knives piercing him, were gone; he no longer experienced a sensation of intense cold; he almost felt that he could lie down in the drifted snow and sleep peacefully. He knew what it would be-- a sleep without end, with the arctic foxes to pick his bones afterward-- and so he resisted the temptation and forced himself onward. The storm still swept straight west from Hudson's Bay, bringing with it endless volleys of snow, round and hard as fine shot, snow that had at first seemed to pierce his flesh and which swished past his feet as if trying to trip him and tossed itself in windrows and mountains in his path. If he could only find timber, shelter! That was what he worked for now. When he had last looked at his watch it was nine o'clock in the morning; now it was late in the afternoon. It might as well have been night. The storm had long since half blinded him. He could not see a dozen paces ahead. But the little life in him still reasoned bravely. It was a heroic spark of life, a fighting spark, and hard to put out. It told him that when he came to shelter he would at least feel it, and that he must fight until the last. The pack on his back held no significance and no weight for him. He might have traveled a mile or ten miles an hour and he would not have sensed the difference. Most men would have buried themselves in the snow and died in comfort, dreaming the pleasant dreams that come as a sort of recompense to the unfortunate who dies of starvation and cold. But the fighting spark commanded Billy to die upon his feet if he died at all. It was this spark which brought him at last to a bit of timber thick enough to give him shelter from wind and snow. It burned a little more warmly then. It flared up and gave him new vision. And then, for the first time, he realized that it must be night. For a light was burning ahead of him, and all else was gloom. His first thought was that it was a campfire miles and miles away. Then it drew nearer, until he knew that it was a light in a cabin window. He dragged himself toward it, and when he came to the door he tried to shout. But no sound fell from his swollen lips. It seemed an hour before he could twist his feet out of his snow-shoes. Then he groped for a latch, pressed against the door, and plunged in.

What he saw was like a picture suddenly revealed for an instant by a flashlight. In the cabin there were four men. Two sat at a table directly in front of him. One held a dice box poised in the air, and had turned a rough, bearded face toward him. The other was a younger man, and in this moment it struck Billy as strange that he should be clutching a can of beans between his hands. A third man stared from where he had been looking down upon the dice-play of the other two. As Billy came in he was in the act of lowering a half-filled bottle from his lips. The fourth man sat on the edge of a bunk, with a face so white and thin that he might have been taken for a corpse if it had not been for the dark glare in his sunken eyes. Billy smelled the odor of whisky; he smelled food. He saw no sign of welcome in the faces turned toward him, but he advanced upon them, mumbling incoherently. And then the spark, the fighting spark in him, gave out, and he crumpled down on the floor. He heard a voice which came to him from a great distance, and which said, "Who the hell is this?" and then, after what seemed to be a long time, he heard that same voice say, "Pitch him back into the snow."

After that he lost consciousness. But in that last moment between light and darkness he experienced a strange thrill that made him want to spring to his feet, for it seemed to him that he had recognized the voice that had said "Pitch him back into the snow."

XXII
INTO THE SOUTH

A long time before he awoke Billy knew that he was not in the snow, and that hot stuff was running down his throat. When he opened his eyes there was no longer a light burning in the cabin. It was day. He felt strangely comfortable, but there was thing in the cabin that stirred him from his rest. It was the odor of frying bacon. All of his hunger had come back. The joy of life, of anticipation, shone in his thin face as he pulled himself up. Another face-- the bearded face-- red-eyed, almost animal-like in its fierce questioning, bent over him.

"Where's your grub, pardner?"

The question was like a stab. Billy did not hear his own voice as he explained.

"Got none!" The bearded man's voice was like a bellow as he turned upon the others, "He's got no grub!"

In that moment Billy choked back the cry on his lips. He knew the voice now-- and the man. It was Bucky Smith! He half rose to his feet and then dropped back. Bucky had not recognized him. His own beard, shaggy hair, and pinched face had saved him from recognition. Fate had played his way.

"We'll divvy up, Bucky," came a weak voice. It was from the thin, white-faced man who had sat corpselike on the edge of his bunk the night before.

"Divvy hell!" growled the other. "It's up to you-- you 'n' Sweedy. You're to blame!"

You're to blame!

The words struck upon Billy's ears with a chill of horror. Starvation was in the cabin. He had fallen among animals instead of men. He saw the thin-faced man who had spoken for him sitting again on the edge of his bunk. Mutely he looked to the others to see who was Sweedy. He was the young man who had clutched the can of beans. It was he who was frying bacon over the sheet-iron stove.

"We'll divvy, Henry and I," he said. "I told you that last night." He looked over at Billy. "Glad you're better," he greeted. "You see, you've struck us at a bad time. We're on our last legs for grub. Our two Indians went out to hunt a week ago and never came back. They're dead, or gone, and we're as good as dead if the storm doesn't let up pretty soon. You can have some of our grub-- Henry's and mine."

It was a cold invitation, lacking warmth or sympathy, and Billy felt that even this man wished that he had died before he reached the cabin. But the man was human; he had at least not cast his voice with the one that had wanted to throw him back into the snow, and he tried to voice his gratitude and at the same time to hide his hunger. He saw that there were three thin slices of bacon in the frying-pan, and it struck him that it would be bad taste to reveal a starvation appetite in the face of such famine. Bucky was looking straight at him as he limped to his feet, and he was sure now that the man he had driven from the Service had not recognized him. He approached Sweedy.

"You saved my life," he said, holding out a hand. "Will you shake ?"

Sweedy shook hands limply.

"It's hell," he said, in a low voice. "We'd have had beans this morning if I hadn't shook dice with him last night." He nodded toward Bucky, who was cutting open the top of a can. "He won!"

"My God--" began Billy.

He didn't finish. Sweedy turned the meat, and added:

"He won a square meal off me yesterday-- a quarter of a pound of bacon. Day before that he won Henry's last can of beans. He's got his share under his blanket over there, and swears he'll shoot any one who goes to monkeyin' with his bed-- so you'd better fight shy of it. Thompson-- he isn't up yet-- chose the whisky for his share, so you'd better fight shy of him, too. Henry and I'll divvy up with you."

"Thanks," said Billy, the one word choking him.

Henry came from his bunk, bent and wabbling. He looked like a dying man, and for the first time Billy noticed that his hair was gray. He was a little man, and his thin hands shook as he held them out over the stove and nodded to Billy. Bucky had opened his can, and approached the stove with a pan of water, coming in beside Billy without noticing him. He brought with him a foul odor of stale tobacco smoke and whisky. After he had put his water over the fire he turned to one of the bunks and with half a dozen coarse epithets roused Thompson, who sat up stupidly, still half drunk. Henry had gone to a small table, and Sweedy followed him with the bacon. Billy did not move. He forgot his hunger. His pulse was beating quickly. Sensations filled him which he had never known or imagined before. Was it possible that these were people of his own kind? Had a madness of some sort driven all human instincts from them? He saw Thompson's red eyes fastened upon him, and he turned his face to escape their questioning, stupid leer. Bucky was turning out the can of beans he had won. Beyond him the door creaked, and Billy heard the wail of the storm. It came to him now as a friendly sort of sound.

"Better draw up, pardner," he heard Sweedy say. "Here's your share."

One of the thin slices of bacon and a hard biscuit were waiting for him on a tin plate. He ate as ravenously as Henry and Sweedy, and drank a cup of hot tea. In two minutes the meal was over. It was terribly inadequate. The few mouthfuls of food stirred up all his craving, and he found it impossible to keep his eyes from Bucky Smith and his beans. Bucky was the only one who seemed well fed, and his horror increased when Henry bent over him and said, in a low whisper: "He didn't get my beans fair. I had three aces and a pair, of deuces, an' he took it on three fives and two sixes. When I objected he called me a liar an' hit me. Them's my beans, or Sweedy's!" There was something almost like murder in the little man's red eyes.

Billy remained silent. He did not care to talk or question. No one asked him who he was or whence he came, and he felt no inclination to know more of the men he had fallen among. Bucky finished, wiped his mouth with his hand, and looked across at Billy.

"How about going out with me to get some wood?" he demanded.

"I'm ready," replied Billy.

For the first time he took notice of himself. He was lame and sickeningly weak, but apparently sound in other ways. The intense cold had not frozen his ears or feet. He put on his heavy moccasins, his thick coat and fur cap, and followed Bucky to the door. He was filled with a strange uneasiness. He was sure that his old enemy had not recognized him, and yet he felt that recognition might come at any moment. If Bucky recognized him-- when they were out alone--

He was not afraid, but he shivered. He was too weak to put up a fight. He did not catch the ugly leer which Bucky turned upon Thompson. But Henry did, and his little eyes grew smaller and blacker. On snow-shoes the two men went out into the storm, Bucky carrying an ax. He led the way through the bit of thin timber, and across a wide open over which the storm swept so fiercely that their trail was covered behind them as they traveled. Billy figured that they had gone a quarter of a mile when they came to the edge of a ravine so steep that it was almost a precipice. For the first time Bucky touched him. He seized him by the arm, and in his voice there was an inhuman, taunting triumph.

"Didn't think I knew you, did you, Billy?" he asked. "Well, I did, and I've just been waiting to get you out alone. Remember my promise, Billy ? I've changed my mind since then. I ain't going to kill you. It's too risky. It's safer to let you die-- by yourself-- as you're goin' to die to-day or to-night. If you come back to the cabin-- I'll shoot you!"

With a movement so quick that Billy had no chance to prepare himself for it Bucky sent him plunging headlong down the side of the ravine. The deep snow saved him in the long fall. For a few moments Billy lay stunned. Then he staggered to his feet and looked up. Bucky was gone. His first thought was to return to the cabin. He could easily find it and confront Bucky there before the others. And yet he did not move. His inclination to go back grew less and less, and after a brief hesitation he made up his mind to continue the struggle for life by himself. After all, his situation would not be much more desperate than that of the men he was leaving behind in the cabin. He buttoned himself up closely, saw that his snow-shoes were securely fastened, and climbed the opposite side of the ridge.

The timber thinned out again, and Billy struck out boldly into the low bush. As he went he wondered what would happen in the cabin. He believed that Henry, of the four, would not pull through alive, and that Bucky would come out best. It was not until the following summer that he learned the facts of Henry's madness, and of the terrible manner in which he avenged himself on Bucky Smith by sticking a knife under the latter's ribs.

Billy now found himself in a position to measure the amount of energy contained in a slice of bacon and a cold biscuit. It was not much. Long before noon his old weakness was upon him again. He found even greater difficulty in dragging his feet over the snow, and it seemed now as though all ambition had left him, and that even the fighting spark was becoming disheartened. He made up his mind to go on until the beginning of night, then he would stop, build a fire, and go to sleep in its warmth.

During the afternoon he passed out of the scrub into a rougher country. His progress was slower, but more comfortable, for at times he found himself protected from the wind. A gloom darker and more somber than that of the storm was falling about him when he came to what appeared to be the end of the Barren country. The earth dropped away from under his feet, and far below him, in a ravine shut out from wind and storm, he saw the black tops of thick spruce. He began to scramble downward. His eyes were no longer fit to judge distance or chance, and he slipped. He slipped a dozen times in the first five minutes, and then there came the time when he did not make a recovery, but plunged down the side of the mountain like a rock. He stopped with a terrific jar, and for the first time during the fall he wanted to cry out with pain. But the voice that he heard did not come from his own lips. It was another voice-- and then two, three, many of them, it seemed to him. His dazed eyes caught glimpses of dark objects floundering in the deep snow about him, and just beyond these objects were four or five tall mounds of snow, like tents, arranged in a circle. He knew what they meant. He had fallen into an Indian camp. In his joy he tried to call out words of greeting, but he had no tongue. Then the floundering figures caught him up, and he was carried to the circle of snow mounds. The last that he knew was that warmth was entering his lungs.

It was a face that he first saw after that, a face that seemed to come to him slowly from out of night, approaching nearer and nearer until he knew that it was a girl's face, with great, dark, strangely shining eyes. In these first moments of his returning consciousness the whimsical thought came to him that he was dying and the face was a part of a pleasant dream. If that were not so, he had fallen at last among friends. His eyes opened wider, he moved, and the face drew back. Movement stimulated returning life, and reason rehabilitated itself in great bounds. In a dozen flashes he went over all that had happened up to the point where he had fallen down the mountain and into the Cree camp. Straight above him he saw the funnel-like peak of a large birch wigwam, and beyond his feet he saw an opening in the birch-bark wall through which there drifted a blue film of smoke. He was in a wigwam. It was warm and exceedingly comfortable. Wondering if he was hurt, he moved. The movement drew a sharp exclamation of pain from him. It was the first real sound he had made, and in an instant the face was over him again. He saw it plainly this time, with its dark eyes and oval cheeks framed between two great braids of black hair. A hand touched his brow, cool and gentle, and a low voice soothed him in half a dozen musical words. The girl was a Cree.

At the sound of her voice an indian woman came up beside the girl, looked down at him for a moment, and then went to the door of the wigwam, speaking in a low voice to some one who was outside. When she returned a man followed in after her. He was old and bent, and his face was thin. His cheek-bones shone, so tightly was the skin drawn over them. Behind him came a younger man, as straight as a tree, with strong shoulders and a head set like a piece of bronze sculpture. This man carried in his hand a frozen fish, which he gave to the woman. As he gave it to her he spoke words in Cree which Billy understood.

"It is the last fish."

For a moment a terrible hand gripped at Billy's heart and almost stopped its beating. He saw the woman take the fish and cut it into two equal parts with a knife, and one of these parts she dropped into a pot of boiling water which hung over the stone fireplace built under the vent in the wall. They were dividing with him their last fish! He made an effort and sat up. The younger man came to him and put a bearskin at his back. He had picked up some of the patois of half-blood French and English.

"You seek," he said, "you hurt-- and hungry! You have eat soon."

He motioned with his hand to the boiling pot. There was not a flicker of animation in his splendid face. There was something god-like in his immobility, something that was awesome in the way he moved and breathed. He sat in silence as the half of the last fish was brought by the girl; and not until Billy stopped eating, choked by the knowledge that he was taking life from these people, did he speak, and then it was to urge him to finish the fish. When he had done, Billy spoke to the Indian in Cree. Instantly the Indian reached over his hand, his face lighting up, and Billy gripped it hard. Mukoki told him what had happened. There had been a camp of twenty-two, and there were now fifteen. Seven had died-- four men, two women, and one child. Each day during the great storm the men had gone out on their futile search for game, and every few days one of them had failed to return. Thus four had died. The dogs were eaten. Corn and fish were gone; there remained but a little flour, and this was for the women and the children. The men had eaten nothing but bark and roots for five days. And there seemed to be no hope. It was death to stray far from camp. That morning two men had set out for the nearest post, but Mukoki said calmly that they would never return.

That night and the next day and the terrible night and day that followed were filled with hours that Billy would never forget. He had sprained one hip badly in his fall, and could not rise from the cot Mukoki was often at his side, his face thinner, his eyes more lusterless. The second day, late in the afternoon, there came a low wailing grief from one of the tepees, a moaning sound that pitched itself to the key of the storm until it seemed to be a part of it. A child had died, and the mother was mourning. That night another of the camp huntsmen failed to return at dusk. But the next day there came at the same time the end of both storm and famine. With dawn the sun shone. And early in the day one of the hunters ran in from the forest nearly crazed with joy. He had ventured farther away than the others, and had found a moose-yard. He had killed two of the animals and brought with him meat for the first feast.

This last great storm of the winter of 1910 passed well into the "break-up" season, and, once the temperature began to rise, the change was swift. Within a week the snow was growing soft underfoot. Two days later Billy hobbled from his cot for the first time. And then, in the passing of a single day and night, the glory of the northern spring burst upon the wilderness. The sun rose warm and golden. From the sides of the mountains and in the valleys water poured forth in rippling, singing floods. The red bakneesh glowed on bared rocks. Moose-birds and jays and wood-thrushes flitted about the camp, and the air was filled with the fragrant smells of new life bursting from earth and tree and shrub.

With return of health and strength Billy's impatience to reach McTabb's cabin grew hourly. He would have set out before his hip was in condition to travel had not Mukoki kept him back. At last the day came when he bade his forest friends good-by and started into the south.

XXIII
AT THE END OF THE TRAIL

The long days and nights of inactivity which Billy had passed in the Indian camp had given him the opportunity to think more calmly of the tragedy which had come into his life, and with returning strength he had drawn himself partly out from the pit of hopelessness and despair into which he had fallen. Deane was dead. Isobel was dead. But the baby Isobel still lived; and in the hope of finding and claiming her for his own he built other dreams for himself out of the ashes of all that had gone for him. He believed that he would find McTabb at the cabin and he would find the child there. So confident had he been that Isobel would live that he had not told McTabb of the uncle who had driven her from the old home in Montreal. He was glad that he had kept this to himself, for there would not be much of a chance of Rookie having found the child's relative. And he made up his mind that he would not give the little Isobel up. He would keep her for himself. He would return to civilization, for he would have her to live for. He would build a home for her, with a garden and dogs and birds and flowers. With his silver-claim money he had fifteen thousand dollars laid away, and she would never know what it meant to be poor. He would educate her and buy her a piano and she would have no end of pretty dresses and things to make her a lady. They would be together and inseparable always, and when she grew up he prayed deep down in his soul that she would be like the older Isobel, her mother.

His grief was deep. He knew that he could never forget, and that the old memories of the wilderness and of the woman he had loved would force themselves upon him, year after year, with their old pain. But these new thoughts and plans for the child made his grief less poignant.

It was late in the afternoon of a day that had been filled with sunlight and the warmth of spring that he came to the Little Beaver, a short distance above McTabb's cabin. He almost ran from there to the clearing, and the sun was just sinking behind the forest in the west when he paused on the edge of the break in the forest and saw the cabin. It was from here that he had last seen little Isobel. The bush behind which he had concealed himself was less than a dozen paces away. He noticed this, and then he observed things which made his heart sink in a strange, cold way. A path had led into the forest at the point where he stood. Now it was almost obliterated by a tangle of last year's weeds and plants. Rookie must have made a new path, he thought. And then, fearfully, he looked about the clearing and at the cabin. Everywhere there was the air of desolation. There was no smoke rising from the chimney. The door was closed. There were no evidences of life outside. Not the sound of a dog, of a laugh, or of a voice broke the dead stillness.

Scarcely breathing, Billy advanced, his heart choked more and more by the fear that gripped him. The door to the cabin was not barred. He opened it. There was nothing inside. The old stove was broken. The bare cots had not been used for months-- perhaps for two years. As he took another step an ermine scampered away ahead of him. He heard the mouselike squeal of its young a moment later under the sapling floor. He went back to the door and stood in the open.

"My God!" he moaned.

He looked in the direction of Couchée's cabin, where Isobel had died. Was there a chance there, he wondered? There was little hope, but he started quickly over the old trail. The gloom of evening fell swiftly about him. It was almost dark when he reached the other clearing. And again his voice broke in a groaning cry. There was no cabin here. McTabb had burned it after the passing of the plague. Where it had stood was now a black and charred mass, already partly covered by the verdure of the wilderness. Billy gripped his hands hard and walked back from it searchingly. A few steps away he found what McTabb had told him that he would find, a mound and a sapling cross. And then, in spite of all the fighting strength that was in him, he flung himself down upon Isobel's grave, and a great, broken cry of grief burst from his lips.

When he raised his head a long time afterward the stars were shimmering in the sky. It was a wonderfully still night, and all that he could hear was the ripple and song of the spring floods in the Little Beaver. He rose silently to his feet and stood for a few moments as motionless as a statue over the grave. Then he turned and went back over the old trail, and from the edge of the clearing he looked back and whispered to himself and to her:

"I'll come back for you, Isobel. I'll come back."

At McTabb's cabin he had left his pack. He put the straps over his shoulder and started south again. There was but one move for him to make now. McTabb was known at Le Pas. He got his supplies and sold his furs there. Some one at Le Pas would know where he had gone with little Isobel.

Not until he was several miles distant from the scene of death and his own broken hopes did he spread out his blanket and lie down for the night. He was up and had breakfast at dawn. On the fourth day he came to the little wilderness out-post-- the end of rail-- on the Saskatchewan. Within an hour he discovered that Rookie McTabb had not been to Le Pas for nearly two years. No one had seen him with a child. That same night a construction train was leaving for Etomami, down on the main line, and Billy lost no time in making up his mind what he would do. He would go to Montreal. If little Isobel was not there she was still somewhere in the wilderness with McTabb. Then he would return, and he would find her if it took him a lifetime.

Days and nights of travel followed, and during those days and nights Billy prayed that he would not find her in Montreal. If by some chance McTabb had discovered her relatives, if Isobel had revealed her secret to him before she died, his last hope in life was gone. He did not think of wasting time in the purchase of new clothes. That would have meant the missing of a train. He still wore his wilderness outfit, even to his fur cap. As he traveled farther eastward people began to regard him curiously. He got the porter to shave off his beard. But his hair was long. His moccasins and German socks were ragged and torn, and there were rents in his caribou-skin coat and his heavy Hudson's Bay sweater-shirt. The hardships he had gone through had left their lines in his face. There was something about him, outside of his strange attire, that made men look at him more than once. Women, more keenly observant than the men, saw the deep-seated grief in his eyes. As he approached Montreal he kept himself more and more aloof from the others.

When at last the train came to a stop at the big station in the heart of the city he walked through the gates and strode up the hill toward Mount Royal. It was an hour or more past noon, and he had eaten nothing since morning. But he had no thought of hunger. Twenty minutes later he was at the foot of the street on which Isobel had told him that she had lived. One by one he passed the old houses of brick and stone, sheltered behind their solid walls. There had been no change in the years since he had been there. Half-way up the hill to the base of the mountain he saw an old gardener trimming ivy about an ancient cannon near a driveway. He stopped and asked:

"Can you tell me where Geoffrey Renaud lives?"

The old gardener looked at him curiously for a moment without speaking. Then he said:

"Renaud? Geoffrey Renaud? That is his house up there behind the red-sand-stone wall. Is it the house you want to see-- or Renaud?"

"Both," said Billy.

"Geoffrey Renaud has been dead for three years," informed the gardener. "Are you a-- relative?"

"No, no," cried Billy, trying to keep his voice steady as he asked the next question. "There are others there. Who are they?"

The old man shook his head.

"I don't know."

"There is a little girl there-- four-- five years old, with golden hair--"

"She was playing in the garden when I came along a few moments ago," replied the gardener. "I heard her-- with the dog--"

Billy waited to hear no more. Thanking his informant, he walked swiftly up the hill to the red-sandstone wall. Before he came to the rusted iron gate he, too, heard a child's laughter, and it set his heart beating wildly. It was just over the wall. In his eagerness he thrust the toe of his moccasined foot into a break in the stone and drew himself up. He looked down into a great garden, and a dozen steps away, close to a thick clump of shrubbery, he saw a child playing with a little puppy. The sun gleamed in her golden hair. He heard her joyous laughter; and then, for an instant, her face was turned toward him.

In that moment he forgot everything, and with a great, glad cry he drew himself up and sprang to the ground on the other side.

"Isobel-- Isobel-- my little Isobel!"

He was beside her, on his knees, with her in his hungry arms, and for a brief space the child was so frightened that she held her breath and stared at him without a sound.

"Don't you know me-- don't you know me--" he almost sobbed. "Little Mystery-- Isobel--"

He heard a sound, a strange, stifled cry, and he looked up. From behind the shrubbery there had come a woman, and she was staring at Billy MacVeigh with a face as white as chalk. He staggered to his feet, and he believed that at last he had gone mad. For it was the vision of Isobel Deane that he saw there, and her blue eyes were glowing at him as he had seen them for an instant that night a long time ago on the edge of the Barren. He could not speak. And then, as he staggered another step back toward the wall, he held out his ragged arms, without knowing what he was doing, and called her name as he had spoken it a hundred times at night beside his lonely campfires. Starvation, his injury, weeks of illness, and his almost superhuman struggle to reach McTabb's cabin, and after that civilization, had consumed his last strength. For days he had lived on the reserve forces of a nervous energy that slipped away from him now, leaving him dizzy and swaying. He fought to overcome the weakness that seemed to have taken the last ounce of strength from his exhausted body, but in spite of his strongest efforts the sunlit garden suddenly darkened before his eyes. In that moment the vision became real, and as he turned toward the wall Isobel Deane called him by name; and in another moment she was at his side, clutching him almost fiercely by the arms and calling him by name over and over again. The weakness and dizziness passed from him in a moment, but in that space he seemed only to realize that he must get back-- over the wall.

"I wouldn't have come-- but-- I-- I-- thought you were-- dead," he said. "They told me-- you were dead. I'm glad-- glad-- but I wouldn't have come--"

She felt the weight of him for an instant on her arm. She knew the things that were in his face-- starvation, pain, the signs of ravage left behind by fever. In these moments Billy did not see the wonderful look that had come into her own face or the wonderful glow in her eyes.

"It was Indian Joe's mother who died," he heard her say. "And since then we have been waiting-- waiting-- waiting-- little Isobel and I. I went away north, to David's grave, and I saw what you had done, and what you had burned into the wood. Some day, I knew, you'd come back to me. We've been waiting-- for you--"

Her voice was barely more than a whisper, but Billy heard it; and all at once his dizziness was gone, and he saw the sunlight shining in Isobel's bright hair and the look in her face and eyes.

"I'm sorry-- sorry-- so sorry I said what I did-- about you-- killing him," she went on. "You remember-- I said that if I got well--"

"Yes--"

"And you thought I meant that if I got well you should go away-- and you promised-- and kept your promise. But I couldn't finish. It didn't seem right-- then. I wanted to tell you-- out there-- that I was sorry-- and that if I got well you could come to me again-- some day somewhere-- and then--"

"Isobel!"

"And now-- you may tell me again what you told me out on the Barren-- a long time ago."

"Isobel-- Isobel--"

"You understand"-- she spoke softly-- "you understand, it cannot happen now-- perhaps not for another year. But now"-- she drew a little nearer-- "you may kiss me," she said. "And then you must kiss little Isobel. And we don't want you to go very far away again. It's lonely-- terribly lonely all by ourselves in the city-- and we're glad you've come-- so glad--"

Her voice broke to a sobbing whisper, and as Billy opened his great, ragged arms and caught her to him he heard that whisper again, saying, "We're glad-- glad-- glad you've come back to us."

"And I-- may-- stay?"

She raised her face, glorious in its welcome.

"If you want me-- still."

At last he believed. But he could not speak. He bent his face to hers, and for a moment they stood thus, while from behind the shrubbery came the sound of little Isobel's joyous laughter.

The Codes Of Hammurabi And Moses
W. W. Davies

QTY

The discovery of the Hammurabi Code is one of the greatest achievements of archaeology, and is of paramount interest, not only to the student of the Bible, but also to all those interested in ancient history...

Religion   **ISBN: *1-59462-338-4***   **Pages:132**
MSRP *$12.95*

The Theory of Moral Sentiments
Adam Smith

QTY

This work from 1749. contains original theories of conscience amd moral judgment and it is the foundation for systemof morals.

Philosophy   ISBN: *1-59462-777-0*   **Pages:536**
MSRP *$19.95*

Jessica's First Prayer
Hesba Stretton

QTY

In a screened and secluded corner of one of the many railway-bridges which span the streets of London there could be seen a few years ago, from five o'clock every morning until half past eight, a tidily set-out coffee-stall, consisting of a trestle and board, upon which stood two large tin cans, with a small fire of charcoal burning under each so as to keep the coffee boiling during the early hours of the morning when the work-people were thronging into the city on their way to their daily toil...

Pages:84

Childrens   ISBN: *1-59462-373-2*   **MSRP *$9.95***

My Life and Work
Henry Ford

QTY

Henry Ford revolutionized the world with his implementation of mass production for the Model T automobile. Gain valuable business insight into his life and work with his own auto-biography... "We have only started on our development of our country we have not as yet, with all our talk of wonderful progress, done more than scratch the surface. The progress has been wonderful enough but..."

Pages:300

Biographies/   ISBN: *1-59462-198-5*   **MSRP *$21.95***

The Art of Cross-Examination
Francis Wellman

QTY

I presume it is the experience of every author, after his first book is published upon an important subject, to be almost overwhelmed with a wealth of ideas and illustrations which could readily have been included in his book, and which to his own mind, at least, seem to make a second edition inevitable. Such certainly was the case with me; and when the first edition had reached its sixth impression in five months, I rejoiced to learn that it seemed to my publishers that the book had met with a sufficiently favorable reception to justify a second and considerably enlarged edition. ..

Pages:412

Reference   **ISBN:** *1-59462-647-2*   *MSRP $19.95*

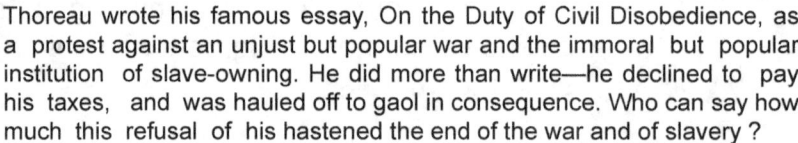

On the Duty of Civil Disobedience
Henry David Thoreau

QTY

Thoreau wrote his famous essay, On the Duty of Civil Disobedience, as a protest against an unjust but popular war and the immoral but popular institution of slave-owning. He did more than write—he declined to pay his taxes, and was hauled off to gaol in consequence. Who can say how much this refusal of his hastened the end of the war and of slavery ?

Law   **ISBN:** *1-59462-747-9*   **Pages:48**

MSRP $7.45

Dream Psychology
Psychoanalysis for Beginners

Sigmund Freud

Dream Psychology Psychoanalysis for Beginners
Sigmund Freud

QTY

Sigmund Freud, born Sigismund Schlomo Freud (May 6, 1856 - September 23, 1939), was a Jewish-Austrian neurologist and psychiatrist who co-founded the psychoanalytic school of psychology. Freud is best known for his theories of the unconscious mind, especially involving the mechanism of repression; his redefinition of sexual desire as mobile and directed towards a wide variety of objects; and his therapeutic techniques, especially his understanding of transference in the therapeutic relationship and the presumed value of dreams as sources of insight into unconscious desires.

Pages:196

Psychology   **ISBN:** *1-59462-905-6*   *MSRP $15.45*

The Miracle of Right Thought
Orison Swett Marden

QTY

Believe with all of your heart that you will do what you were made to do. When the mind has once formed the habit of holding cheerful, happy, prosperous pictures, it will not be easy to form the opposite habit. It does not matter how improbable or how far away this realization may see, or how dark the prospects may be, if we visualize them as best we can, as vividly as possible, hold tenaciously to them and vigorously struggle to attain them, they will gradually become actualized, realized in the life. But a desire, a longing without endeavor, a yearning abandoned or held indifferently will vanish without realization.

Pages:360

Self Help   **ISBN:** *1-59462-644-8*   *MSRP $25.45*

QTY

The Rosicrucian Cosmo-Conception Mystic Christianity *by Max Heindel*   ISBN: *1-59462-188-8* **$38.95**
The Rosicrucian Cosmo-conception is not dogmatic, neither does it appeal to any other authority than the reason of the student. It is: not controversial, but is: sent forth in the, hope that it may help to clear...   New Age/Religion Pages 646

Abandonment To Divine Providence *by Jean-Pierre de Caussade*   ISBN: *1-59462-228-0* **$25.95**
"The Rev. Jean Pierre de Caussade was one of the most remarkable spiritual writers of the Society of Jesus in France in the 18th Century. His death took place at Toulouse in 1751. His works have gone through many editions and have been republished...   Inspirational/Religion Pages 400

Mental Chemistry *by Charles Haanel*   ISBN: *1-59462-192-6* **$23.95**
Mental Chemistry allows the change of material conditions by combining and appropriately utilizing the power of the mind. Much like applied chemistry creates something new and unique out of careful combinations of chemicals the mastery of mental chemistry...   New Age Pages 354

The Letters of Robert Browning and Elizabeth Barret Barrett 1845-1846 vol II   ISBN: *1-59462-193-4* **$35.95**
by Robert Browning and Elizabeth Barrett   Biographies Pages 596

Gleanings In Genesis (volume I) *by Arthur W. Pink*   ISBN: *1-59462-130-6* **$27.45**
Appropriately has Genesis been termed "the seed plot of the Bible" for in it we have, in germ form, almost all of the great doctrines which are afterwards fully developed in the books of Scripture which follow...   Religion/Inspirational Pages 420

The Master Key *by L. W. de Laurence*   ISBN: *1-59462-001-6* **$30.95**
In no branch of human knowledge has there been a more lively increase of the spirit of research during the past few years than in the study of Psychology, Concentration and Mental Discipline. The requests for authentic lessons in Thought Control, Mental Discipline and...   New Age/Business Pages 422

The Lesser Key Of Solomon Goetia *by L. W. de Laurence*   ISBN: *1-59462-092-X* **$9.95**
This translation of the first book of the "Lernegton" which is now for the first time made accessible to students of Talismanic Magic was done, after careful collation and edition, from numerous Ancient Manuscripts in Hebrew, Latin, and French...   New Age/Occult Pages 92

Rubaiyat Of Omar Khayyam *by Edward Fitzgerald*   ISBN:*1-59462-332-5* **$13.95**
Edward Fitzgerald, whom the world has already learned, in spite of his own efforts to remain within the shadow of anonymity, to look upon as one of the rarest poets of the century, was born at Bredfield, in Suffolk, on the 31st of March, 1809. He was the third son of John Purcell...   Music Pages 172

Ancient Law *by Henry Maine*   ISBN: *1-59462-128-4* **$29.95**
The chief object of the following pages is to indicate some of the earliest ideas of mankind, as they are reflected in Ancient Law, and to point out the relation of those ideas to modern thought.   Religion/History Pages 452

Far-Away Stories *by William J. Locke*   ISBN: *1-59462-129-2* **$19.45**
"Good wine needs no bush, but a collection of mixed vintages does. And this book is just such a collection. Some of the stories I do not want to remain buried for ever in the museum files of dead magazine-numbers an author's not unpardonable vanity..."   Fiction Pages 272

Life of David Crockett *by David Crockett*   ISBN: *1-59462-250-7* **$27.45**
"Colonel David Crockett was one of the most remarkable men of the times in which he lived. Born in humble life, but gifted with a strong will, an indomitable courage, and unremitting perseverance...   Biographies/New Age Pages 424

Lip-Reading *by Edward Nitchie*   ISBN: *1-59462-206-X* **$25.95**
Edward B. Nitchie, founder of the New York School for the Hard of Hearing, now the Nitchie School of Lip-Reading, Inc, wrote "LIP-READING Principles and Practice". The development and perfecting of this meritorious work on lip-reading was an undertaking...   How-to Pages 400

A Handbook of Suggestive Therapeutics, Applied Hypnotism, Psychic Science   ISBN: *1-59462-214-0* **$24.95**
by Henry Munro   Health/New Age/Health/Self-help Pages 376

A Doll's House: and Two Other Plays *by Henrik Ibsen*   ISBN: *1-59462-112-8* **$19.95**
Henrik Ibsen created this classic when in revolutionary 1848 Rome. Introducing some striking concepts in playwriting for the realist genre, this play has been studied the world over.   Fiction/Classics/Plays 308

The Light of Asia *by sir Edwin Arnold*   ISBN: *1-59462-204-3* **$13.95**
In this poetic masterpiece, Edwin Arnold describes the life and teachings of Buddha. The man who was to become known as Buddha to the world was born as Prince Gautama of India but he rejected the worldly riches and abandoned the reigns of power when...   Religion/History/Biographies Pages 170

The Complete Works of Guy de Maupassant *by Guy de Maupassant*   ISBN: *1-59462-157-8* **$16.95**
"For days and days, nights and nights, I had dreamed of that first kiss which was to consecrate our engagement, and I knew not on what spot I should put my lips..."   Fiction/Classics Pages 240

The Art of Cross-Examination *by Francis L. Wellman*   ISBN: *1-59462-309-0* **$26.95**
Written by a renowned trial lawyer, Wellman imparts his experience and uses case studies to explain how to use psychology to extract desired information through questioning.   How-to/Science/Reference Pages 408

Answered or Unanswered? *by Louisa Vaughan*   ISBN: *1-59462-248-5* **$10.95**
Miracles of Faith in China   Religion Pages 112

The Edinburgh Lectures on Mental Science (1909) *by Thomas*   ISBN: *1-59462-008-3* **$11.95**
This book contains the substance of a course of lectures recently given by the writer in the Queen Street Hail, Edinburgh. Its purpose is to indicate the Natural Principles governing the relation between Mental Action and Material Conditions...   New Age Psychology Pages 148

Ayesha *by H. Rider Haggard*   ISBN: *1-59462-301-5* **$24.95**
Verily and indeed it is the unexpected that happens! Probably if there was one person upon the earth from whom the Editor of this, and of a certain previous history, did not expect to hear again...   Classics Pages 380

Ayala's Angel *by Anthony Trollope*   ISBN: *1-59462-352-X* **$29.95**
The two girls were both pretty, but Lucy who was twenty-one who supposed to be simple and comparatively unattractive, whereas Ayala was credited, as her Bombwhat romantic name might show, with poetic charm and a taste for romance. Ayala when her father died was nineteen...   Fiction Pages 484

The American Commonwealth *by James Bryce*   ISBN: *1-59462-286-8* **$34.45**
An interpretation of American democratic political theory. It examines political mechanics and society from the perspective of Scotsman James Bryce   Politics Pages 572

Stories of the Pilgrims *by Margaret P. Pumphrey*   ISBN: *1-59462-116-0* **$17.95**
This book explores pilgrims religious oppression in England as well as their escape to Holland and eventual crossing to America on the Mayflower, and their early days in New England...   History Pages 268

QTY

The Fasting Cure *by Sinclair Upton*　　　　　　　　　　　ISBN: *1-59462-222-1*　**$13.95**
In the Cosmopolitan Magazine for May, 1910, and in the Contemporary Review (London) for April, 1910, I published an article dealing with my experiences in fasting. I have written a great many magazine articles, but never one which attracted so much attention... New Age/Self Help/Health Pages 164

Hebrew Astrology *by Sepharial*　　　　　　　　　　　　ISBN: *1-59462-308-2*　**$13.45**
In these days of advanced thinking it is a matter of common observation that we have left many of the old landmarks behind and that we are now pressing forward to greater heights and to a wider horizon than that which represented the mind-content of our progenitors... Astrology Pages 144

Thought Vibration or The Law of Attraction in the Thought World　　　ISBN: *1-59462-127-6*　**$12.95**
by William Walker Atkinson　　　　　　　　　　　　　　　Psychology/Religion Pages 144

Optimism *by Helen Keller*　　　　　　　　　　　　　　ISBN: *1-59462-108-X*　**$15.95**
Helen Keller was blind, deaf, and mute since 19 months old, yet famously learned how to overcome these handicaps, communicate with the world, and spread her lectures promoting optimism. An inspiring read for everyone... Biographies/Inspirational Pages 84

Sara Crewe *by Frances Burnett*　　　　　　　　　　　　ISBN: *1-59462-360-0*　**$9.45**
In the first place, Miss Minchin lived in London. Her home was a large, dull, tall one, in a large, dull square, where all the houses were alike, and all the sparrows were alike, and where all the door-knockers made the same heavy sound... Childrens/Classic Pages 88

The Autobiography of Benjamin Franklin *by Benjamin Franklin*　　ISBN: *1-59462-135-7*　**$24.95**
The Autobiography of Benjamin Franklin has probably been more extensively read than any other American historical work, and no other book of its kind has had such ups and downs of fortune. Franklin lived for many years in England, where he was agent... Biographies/History Pages 332

Name	
Email	
Telephone	
Address	
City, State ZIP	

☐ **Credit Card**　　　　☐ **Check / Money Order**

Credit Card Number	
Expiration Date	
Signature	

Please Mail to:　Book Jungle
　　　　　　　　　PO Box 2226
　　　　　　　　　Champaign, IL 61825
or Fax to:　　　630-214-0564

ORDERING INFORMATION

web: *www.bookjungle.com*
email: *sales@bookjungle.com*
fax: *630-214-0564*
mail: *Book Jungle PO Box 2226 Champaign, IL 61825*
or PayPal *to sales@bookjungle.com*

Please contact us for bulk discounts

DIRECT-ORDER TERMS

**20% Discount if You Order
Two or More Books**
Free Domestic Shipping!
Accepted: Master Card, Visa,
Discover, American Express

www.ingramcontent.com/pod-product-compliance
Lightning Source LLC
Chambersburg PA
CBHW080822020726
47501CB00009B/2388